A Village Fete MURDER

BOOKS BY KATIE GAYLE

Julia Bird Mysteries

An English Garden Murder

Murder in the Library

Epiphany Bloom Mysteries

The Kensington Kidnap

The Museum Murder

Death at the Gates

A Village Fete MURDER

KATIE GAYLE

bookouture

Published by Bookouture in 2023

An imprint of Storyfire Ltd.
Carmelite House
50 Victoria Embankment
London EC4Y 0DZ

www.bookouture.com

ISBN: 978-1-80314-898-4
eBook ISBN: 978-1-80314-897-7

To the readers who make it all worthwhile!

1

Julia peeped into the oven. The cake looked magnificent. Spongy and chocolatey and delicious, just as the recipe – for Delicious Foolproof Chocolate Sponge – had promised.

Julia always thought the term foolproof sounded like a challenge. She imagined rising to her full height of almost five foot six, placing hands on hips and saying, 'Foolproof, you say? Well, we'll see about that. You haven't met *this* fool!'

Julia's baking history was littered with chewy meringues, crumbling scones and mysteriously indented Victoria sponges. She had learned humility the hard way, and now actively looked for the word 'foolproof' and its cousin 'flop-proof'.

It had certainly paid off this time, she thought, inhaling the rich fresh-baked smell of the moist and shapely cake that was filling her kitchen in the wan afternoon light.

Jake – her Labrador, who was, in fact, the exact colour of the Delicious Foolproof Chocolate Sponge – looked at her expectantly. This was no time to be baking, in his view. This was time to be out and about, investigating the river path for interesting smells, friendly dogs and those dastardly ducks that needed keeping in line.

'Five minutes,' she said. 'I'll take the cake out and we can have our walk while it's cooling.'

Jake gave her a look that indicated he was prepared to be patient, but wasn't delighted about it. Julia opened the kitchen door and waved a kitchen cloth to shoo him out. 'Go on into the garden, I'll be there in a minute.'

The success of her baking project was particularly pleasing because it was destined for a competition at the Berrywick Spring Fair being held the next day. It would be Julia's first experience of the fair, as she had only moved to the village the previous summer. Putting together what she'd heard around the village, it sounded to be something between the Queen's Jubilee and the local farmers' market, with a dash of *Great British Bake Off* and a bit of old-fashioned fun fair thrown in. It was hosted in the grounds of Berrywick House, the grand estate two miles from the village, and visitors came from all over to enjoy the festivities.

The bakers in the village had been asked to each bake a cake for the Women's Institute stall. The cakes were to be sold, with the proceeds going to the WI, but before they were sold, they would be lined up on display, and prizes awarded for decoration. Julia, it must be said, had no expectation of winning the cake decorating competition. Her friend, Tabitha, had described some of the more ambitious of the previous year's entrants – a Mad Hatter's hat, a country garden ablaze with icing flowers, a multi-coloured architectural wonder based on the water slide of the nearby water park.

Julia wasn't in that league of lunacy. Her modest expectation was that she would make a tasty cake that someone would buy and enjoy for tea, and a few pounds would go to the WI. Her decorating efforts would consist of icing the Delicious Foolproof Chocolate Sponge in the morning, and prettying it up with the fancy sprinkles she'd bought for the occasion.

Julia glanced out of the kitchen window. The light was

fading fast. If Jake was to have his walk, they'd have to hurry. The peaceful twilight scene was interrupted by a flash of gold, followed by a dark brown blur. Julia couldn't believe her eyes – the gold flash was one of her hens; the brown blur was Jake.

'Jake,' she yelled, banging on the window. He ignored her, bounding cheerfully after the hysterical chicken.

How had the chicken got out of the coop, she wondered, as she turned and ran for the kitchen door. That question answered itself as soon as she got outside. The door to the coop was swinging open. She must have not locked it properly after she'd fed them in the morning. She noted with relief that the rest of the flock had sensibly taken cover behind the laying boxes, having seen how their companion was faring in the big wide world.

'Jake,' she bellowed at the brown blur. 'Come in.'

He slowed and looked at her, torn between obedience to his mistress's orders, and the delight of the chase. It had to be said that her patient dog-training was finally paying off. The puppy who had failed guide dog school was mostly fairly well behaved. Unless there was a bird in his field of vision. Ducks, geese, pigeons – he couldn't resist chasing them. He'd probably lunge for an ostrich if he had the chance.

She saw the cogs in his doggy brain whirring as he hesitated.

'Come in,' she said in her most calm and authoritative tone, the tone she'd employed to good effect in her years as a social worker for troubled youth. It worked perhaps sixty-five per cent of the time.

Today, Jake was solidly in the remaining thirty-five per cent. He gave her an apologetic look and leapt after the chicken, which had taken the opportunity to dive for cover in the rhododendrons.

Julia charged after him, muttering dire threats and impolite words under her breath.

The chicken had made a smart move – not something she

found herself saying very often – and hidden quietly in the undergrowth. Jake was crashing about randomly, but she could see he was losing interest.

'Get back here,' she said, lunging for him and grabbing his collar. He shot a longing glance over his shoulder at the open coop.

'Don't even think about it,' Julia said in a low, threatening voice. She pointed at the kitchen door and said firmly, 'Basket!'

He slunk off guiltily.

Julia grabbed the chicken food tin from its place outside the door of the coop, and rattled it noisily, calling 'Chook, chook, chook,' in a high sing-song voice. The hens came running, as they always did. The rumpled one, Jake's intended lunch, emerged rather nervously from the rhododendrons and joined them. She tossed a few handfuls of grain into the coop and shut the door firmly, checking the lock was properly in place. She let out a deep sigh and leaned against the wire, getting her breath back and waiting for her heart to slow.

Somewhat calmer now, she inhaled deeply. What was that she could smell? A whiff of something burning.

Something sweet.

Julia set off for the house at a run, Jake bounding merrily out to greet her, bringing with him the unmistakable scent of burnt cake.

2

'Well-behaved dogs on leads welcome,' Sean read, pointing at the sign at the entrance of the fair and giving Julia a wry smile.

'Well, he's a dog, and he'll be on a lead, and that's about all I can say about that,' said Julia with an exaggerated shrug. Sean laughed, took a hand from the steering wheel and patted her knee. She would have put her hand on his, but both hands were currently occupied holding Delicious Foolproof Chocolate Sponge the Second firmly on her lap. Julia was having no more cake disasters. She had started a new round of cake baking at 7 p.m. the previous evening, and had got up at the crack of dawn to ice it, toss sprinkles over the icing and get to the fair for opening time.

Sean followed the signs to the car park and pulled into a parking place. In front of them, Berrywick House was a lovely sight, set on a small rise, its sandstone glowing golden and windows glinting in the morning sun. The lawn in front looked as if each blade of grass had been measured and snipped to a uniform height by elves. On either side were formal gardens of ponds and fountains, hedges and topiaries. A row of tall cypress trees stood sentry to left and right.

'Nice spot,' Julia said. 'I feel like I'm in a BBC production of some Jane Austen novel. We are the poor country cousins arriving at the Big House.'

'In fact, one of those period films was filmed here a few years back,' said Sean. 'Can't remember which one, but it was quite the buzz in the village. A few local people got parts as extras in crowd scenes – peasants and footmen and chambermaids and servants and such.'

'They'd need a lot of those for this place. Imagine keeping the windows clean. Fun for the local would-be actors though. I'd love to see the film. Let's find out what it was called and watch it one evening. See who we can spot.' Julia noticed that she had slipped into a relaxed use of 'we' in the months that she and Sean had been – what, dating? An item? More than friends? She never knew what to call their relationship. And what to call him was even more tricky. Boyfriend was ridiculous – they were in their sixties for goodness' sake – but the word 'partner' always reminded her of a law firm.

'Yes, let's. Ask Nicky, she'll certainly remember what it was called. She was in it. A milkmaid or something, and there was a clear shot of her face.'

'I might be able to convince her to tell me about it,' Julia said. They smiled in mutual acknowledgement of the fact that Nicky was the most talkative over-sharer in the village – against some stiff competition.

A big marquee behind the manor house rather destroyed the Regency period vibe, although it did look festive, festooned with white, green and yellow bunting. Julia could make out the words *Berrywick Spring Fair* in silver about the front entrance.

'Let's go and hand over the cake before there's another disaster,' she said.

Sean got out of the car and walked round to her door to take the cake from her. She got out and took the cake back from him.

After the previous mishap, they both handled it rather nervously, like two bomb disposal experts dealing with a suspicious package. Sean opened the back of the car and put the leads on the dogs – his well-mannered, easy-going, honey-coloured crossbreed, Leo, and Jake, the dastardly cake destroyer. Sean took both leads, and they followed a thin stream of stall-holders and early fair-goers – a few, like Julia, holding a cake for the competition – making their way through the avenue of cypresses to the marquee.

Julia spotted Wilma from Second Chances, the charity shop where Julia volunteered every Wednesday, carrying an enormous flower arrangement. Wilma had talked about nothing else for the last two weeks, so it was lovely to actually see it. Unfortunately, it was so big and unwieldy that Julia had no hope of getting Wilma's attention over it.

As she stood dithering, wondering whether to call out to Wilma, a voice came from behind them.

'Time and tide wait for no dogs. A stitch in my side saves nine trips to the slide.'

'Edna,' said Sean warmly, turning to greet the old woman. 'Good to see you.'

'Not if I see you first,' said Edna, wrapping her collection of shawls and scarves tightly around herself as if Sean might be thinking of stealing them, and walking resolutely past him.

'I do sometimes wonder if she isn't a danger to herself,' said Julia, watching the elderly woman depart at a fast-paced hobble. 'I know that everyone in the village knows her, and keeps an eye, but she does seem to be quite out of it.'

'Better than being in a home,' said Sean, which was what everybody in the village always said when it came to Edna. Julia sighed. It was hard to shake her London social worker ways of thinking about things. But it was true that Edna didn't ever seem to come to any actual harm, or cause it.

A collection of bouncy castles and slides squatted to one

side of the path like some child-friendly, primary-coloured Stonehenge. On the other side, food trucks were setting up next to a field of trestle tables and benches. There was a maypole, its blue and white ribbons fluttering in the breeze, awaiting the dancers. Frank Sinatra crooned 'It Might as Well Be Spring' from a speaker somewhere. Not for the last time that day, Julia suspected.

Julia led the way into the tent, which was divided into stalls. At the entrance, she bumped straight into Tabitha, who was manning a stall for the library. Tabitha had arranged some piles of books around the table, and had a pile of membership forms and pens set out. *Join Your Local Library* urged a banner above the table.

'It looks lovely,' said Julia, after they had exchanged 'hellos'. 'I'm sure you'll get lots of new members.'

Julia's oldest friend smiled. 'Lots is a big aim for a village, city girl. I'll be happy if five people complete the forms.'

Julia laughed. Big city thinking strikes again.

Some stallholders were still putting the finishing touches to their displays – tweaking ribbons and bunting, ensuring that their wares were displayed to maximum viewing pleasure. Signage demarcated the areas – *Local Produce*, *Gifts*, *Easter Fare*, *Clothing*, *Garden* and so on.

It wasn't hard to see where Julia needed to be. A huge table just ahead of her was covered in cakes. At the front of the table, in prime position, was a large green Easter wreath made of individual impeccably iced cupcakes, decorated with edible blossoms and darling little bunnies and sprinkled with edible silver stars and baubles. It was magnificent.

'Look at this lot,' she muttered to Sean as they approached, clutching Delicious Foolproof Chocolate Sponge the Second, which seemed to shrink into itself the closer they got to the table. Its chocolatey, spongy magnificence suddenly looked very ordinary by comparison with the others. An Easter egg-shaped cake. A couple of elaborate bunnies, one the size of a toddler. A huge chocolate nest, decorated with eggs and chicks. A magnificent tray cake decorated to look like a field of flowers and a four-tier rendering of a Cotswold village. There was also a more moderate selection of traditional Easter simnel cakes with balls of marzipan and home-made hot cross buns. Sean hung back with the dogs, for safety's sake, and Julia approached the table.

There appeared to be no one there. Julia dithered for a moment, wondering if she should just leave the cake. But before she could do so, a young woman appeared from behind her, wiping her hands on a candy-striped apron and giving Julia a wide smile. Her name badge said *Candy*, which seemed either preposterously unlikely or just perfect. 'Hello. Sorry to keep you. I'm up and down to the car, still getting set up. You've brought a cake? How lovely, thank you. That's very kind. And doesn't that look delicious?'

'It's chocolate,' Julia said, rather unnecessarily, holding it towards her.

'Everyone loves chocolate, don't they? Hang on a mo...' Candy dug into the front pocket of her apron and took out her iPhone. 'Let me get a photo. I'm photographing all our lovely bakers, aren't I? For social media.'

Julia held up the cake and grinned awkwardly. Candy took the picture before she had a chance to arrange her face into a friendlier smile. Julia knew she'd look like a deer in the headlights in that one. And not a young deer.

'There you go, and don't you look lovely? Pop it down – there's a spot here, I think?' said the young woman, who seemed to speak mostly in questions. 'And all the money for a good cause, did you know?'

Setting it down, Julia was pleased to see that there were plenty of regular cakes behind the showstoppers. Delicious Foolproof Chocolate Sponge the Second seemed to perk up. It looked quite at home amongst them.

'There we go, and won't someone be enjoying it for their tea this afternoon?' Candy paused for a moment and looked from the cake to Julia. 'You know? I might just buy this one myself. There are some fine-looking confections here, but for my money, there's nothing to touch a good, honest chocolate cake, wouldn't you say? And doesn't yours look just the business?'

'Well, thank you. I hope you enjoy it,' Julia said, feeling rather ridiculously pleased with this compliment. She allowed herself a pleasant moment of quiet pride. When she'd moved to Berrywick, her baking game had been non-existent. And now look at her!

'You have a lovely day at the fair, and a happy Easter to you?'

The marquee was starting to fill up with early birds hoping to miss the crowds and catch the metaphorical worm – namely, the perfect trinket or treat or accessory for themselves, or to give to some tricky-to-shop-for relative. Sean and Julia agreed to have a quick look around the stalls before it got too busy. Then they'd take the dogs for a walk in the grounds.

Julia mentally surveyed her shopping list. Jess, her daughter, would be turning twenty-five on the first of June. She'd been born two weeks before Peter's birthday, which meant Peter's birthday was coming up soon too. What was the protocol for gifting to an ex-husband? She'd better get him something. Nothing too personal. A stall offering custom-made food hampers answered her need. Julia selected seeded crackers, a tin of salmon pâté, and a bottle dandelion and burdock, which had been recommended by the bearded proprietor whose gentle face seemed at odds with the tattoos snaking up his neck.

'For a gift?' he asked.

'Yes, a gift for a friend.'

'Good choice,' he said. 'A bit of cheese would round it off nicely. How about English Cotswold?'

'If you say so. What is it?'

'Similar to a Gloucester, with chives and onion. It's traditional to the area. Very good.'

Julia agreed to the cheese and handed over her credit card, pleased to have solved the tricky gifting conundrum so successfully. Her relief was short-lived, however. Next up, Jess was equally tricky, but in a different way. She was living in Hong Kong in what was, she claimed, '*literally* a shoe box, Mum'. There was no room for knick-knacks, and no point in sending them, considering the postage. Or food. Truth was, she'd probably appreciate a few pounds more than anything else.

A few stalls over, Julia picked up a pretty necklace: a silver chain with a tiny coil of stone as a pendant.

'It's an ammonite,' said the stallholder, a young woman with her hair shaved down to an inch and bleached a fierce white gold. She was about the same age as Jess, Julia noted, and had something of Jess about her, although Jess would never have shaved her head or pierced her nose with a ring. 'They used to call them snakestones, but it's a fossilised mollusc, millions of years old. You find them around this area – they're not very rare, but still, a treasure.'

It really was, and Jess would have loved it fifteen years ago, when she was mad for fossils and dinosaurs and all things ancient. But now? Julia didn't know; she hadn't seen her daughter in two years. Julia didn't really know what Jess liked now. Julia looked at the little grey cross-section of a long-dead animal cupped in her palm, and as she so often did where Jess was concerned, she felt a deep pang of indeterminate origin – guilt, love, loss, sadness, longing for what once was. She bought the necklace.

The crowd was swelling by the minute, and even though the aisles were wide, it seemed a matter of time before Jake tripped someone up. And besides, whoever was in charge of the music had ramped up the volume, with a consequent upping of voices. However much one liked listening to 'Summer Nights', the noise was getting a little loud for good cheer. Julia looked at her watch. Perfect timing. She was to meet Sean at noon and it was quarter to.

'Come on, Jakey, let's get out of here and go and find Leo.'

A heavy, sweet scent drew her attention to a flower stall on the way out. It was absolutely brimming with spring blooms. She stopped and looked in awe at the display. Tulips, anemones and peonies were some of the flowers that she recognised, but there were dozens more that she didn't. She closed her eyes and took a deep breath.

A round face emerged from behind the carnations and gave Julia a smile. 'All from around here,' the woman said, straightening up. 'That's why they smell so good. They haven't been in cold storage for weeks on end.'

'They're magnificent. It's hard to choose. I'll take a mixed bunch,' said Julia, looking at a big bucket of them.

'I'll pop them in some damp paper for you, keep them fresh. Here you go. Seven pounds.'

Sean was already at the car, where they'd agreed to meet to deposit any shopping before taking a stroll around the grounds. He looked happy to see her. 'Bit loud for me,' he said. 'But I got a few herbs for the garden.'

They popped their parcels and pots and Julia's bouquet in the boot and set off, skirting the food area, tempted by the smell of crêpes and cinnamon, but not stopping, heading for the gardens and the fields beyond. Once they'd passed the tables and food trucks, it was quieter almost immediately. A few people wandered the paths, most with young children, some with dogs. Julia noticed a woman in a bright green coat, having what seemed to be an intense conversation with her teen son, the woman's arm wrapped protectively around the boy while they spoke. Julia felt a pang of yearning for those years when she had been the centre of Jess's world, the solver of all problems.

From the hill on which the manor house sat, they looked over a patchwork of fields, gold and green, marked out with darker green hedgerows. The river snaked through the fields and into the village of Berrywick. Julia followed it with her eyes, trying to match this aerial view with the paths and roads and woods she and Jake walked every day.

'I think that's a bit of my roof!' she exclaimed. 'Over there, look: that's the footpath to the river, and that must be me on the right there, next to the thatched place.' She felt oddly delighted to have located herself and her new home. It made her feel grounded, somehow. As if she belonged.

'So it is! Well spotted. And mine would be off to the left of the spire, but you can't see it with all the trees in their spring glory.'

They identified a few more places in the dinky village below and beyond them before moving on, coming to a signpost on a wrought-iron post.

'Barn, river or maze?' Sean offered, reading the words on the pointers.

'Maze!' said Julia, without needing to think about it at all. 'Believe it or not, I've never actually been in one. I'd love to give it a go.'

'Ah well, maze it is then,' he said.

'We should have brought a sandwich, or one of those crêpes, in case we can't get out and are stuck for weeks, starving slowly to death.'

'I agree about the crêpes; a grave oversight, in retrospect. But you don't need to worry about dying a lingering death stuck in a maze in the Cotswolds in the era of the mobile phone,' he said.

'Right then. Let's go. Crêpes after, as a reward.'

They took the left fork.

3

Sean and Julia walked through the maze in silence for a while, each engrossed in their own thoughts as they followed the twists and turns of the path. The dogs trotted at their sides on leads. Thick, almost impenetrable holly bushes, neatly cut to a flawless vertical, boxed them in on both sides.

Julia was surprised to discover how cosy it felt in the maze. The thick hedges blocked a chilly breeze. The sky above was a soft, pale blue, with occasional puffy clouds, and a wan English sun doing its best to herald spring. She didn't feel at all claustrophobic or trapped, just happy to wander along, trusting that they'd get somewhere. Her musing on the profound resonance this might have for life – she had, after all, wandered to Berrywick, and found her cottage and Jake and Sean and a new life – was interrupted by Sean saying, 'Left or right?'

'Right,' she said easily, not because she knew, but because it didn't really matter. As Sean had said, it was hard to get into trouble in a maze these days.

'Okay then.'

They turned right.

A few more lefts and rights and they were thoroughly turned about. They stopped.

'It feels as if we need to go more to the left. West, would that be?' Sean said, gesturing in the direction of who knew what.

'I've honestly no idea,' Julia said. 'It feels as if we're close to the centre, I'd say.'

'Let's carry on then.'

Julia dug in her bag. 'No crêpes, but I do have a roll of Rolos. Want one?'

Sean's blue eyes sparkled even more brightly when he saw the chocolates. 'Ooh, yes please.'

Julia dropped Jake's lead and opened the gold wrapping to reveal the first chocolatey mound. She popped it up with her thumb and offered it to Sean, who took it and put it into his mouth with a murmur of appreciation. Jake took the opportunity to trot off down the path of the maze and take a sharp right.

'Jake!' shouted Julia, and took off after him. 'If we lose him in the maze, goodness knows how we'll find him. Damn! Jake! Get back here!'

Sean followed her with Leo, who was enjoying the chase more than either of the humans.

The Lab ran on happily, with Julia just keeping up, but not fast enough to grab the lead. He took a left, then a right. Or was it a right, then a left? Whatever, they followed, puffing and panting. She lost sight of him at each corner, but spotted him again with relief as she rounded it herself. Another turn, and another, the little troop following the big brown dog. It reminded Julia of *The Gingerbread Man*, the book she'd read to Jess as a child: 'Run, run, as fast as you can...' with the whole town in hot pursuit of the naughty spiced fellow.

Her own naughty spiced fellow finally came to a sudden stop. He sat down, his tail wagging, as if he expected to be admired for his athletic performance. Julia bent down and grabbed the lead, then rested her hands on her knees and took a few slow, deep breaths. She heard Sean and Leo come in behind her.

She straightened and glanced up. They were in a square clearing, surrounded on four sides by hedges. In front of her, in the centre of the clearing, was a small fountain. Jake had brought them to the centre of the maze, Julia realised. What a clever chap he really was! 'Can you believe it, Sean? That naughty Jake found the centre!' she said, laughing as she turned to face him.

But Sean was white-faced and silent. Julia followed his gaze to a stone bench to the left of the opening they'd just entered.

On the bench was a woman.

And the woman was dead.

Sean broke his pose of frozen shock and knelt down next to the bench, his fingers already stretched out, seeking the flutter of a pulse. Julia watched in horror as he probed the motionless woman for signs of life. She was seated on the bench as if she'd been taking a rest and dozed off: her body slumped slightly to the left, her head dropped forward at an uncomfortable angle. Her face, however, was pale and mottled with a blueish tinge. Sean held the woman's wrist and then felt at her throat. He listened at her mouth for a hint of breath, and at her chest for the merest heartbeat. Julia's own heart raced. The nails of her clenched fingers dug deeper into her palms as each moment passed. As hope receded.

Sean turned to Julia and shook his head.

Julia reached for her phone and dialled 999, cursing herself for not having done so the moment she saw the body. Not that it would have made any difference, by the look of it. She was almost sure.

The operator answered in seconds, and Julia quickly gave him the details.

'A maze, you say?'

'Yes, a hedge maze at Berrywick House. You should ask the groundsman or someone to assist the officers, there must be a map.'

'Thank you, police officers are on their way.'

The silent phone in her hand, Julia surveyed the dead woman from head to toe. She seemed a few years younger than Julia, mid- to late-fifties perhaps. She wore a lightweight yellow jacket over a pale grey woollen polo neck jumper and light grey trousers. Her feet rested solidly on the ground in their dark grey lace-up walking shoes. Next to her feet was a little basket, the kind you carry over your shoulder. Julie looked in without touching anything. A folded raincoat took up most of the space and blocked her view of the rest of the contents. All Julia could see was the top of a banana and the edge of a water bottle. She felt a pang at the sight of the woman's modest snack. Had she sat down to eat it, and died? There was no sign of a purse or handbag or phone.

'Better leave that for the police,' Sean said, his eyes following hers. They'd been together for less than a year, but he knew Julia well. Which meant he knew that the temptation to take a peek, just for identification purposes, was strong. 'Just in case.'

'There's no sign of...' Julia's voice faltered at the word, and it came out in a thin, wavering question: 'Murder?'

'Not that I can see. It looks like a sudden heart attack, or perhaps an embolism, but the police and the coroner will have to make that determination. Best not to touch anything.'

Julia was relieved that Sean didn't think there was foul play. In the past year, she had seen more dead bodies than anyone should see in a lifetime. Julia had had more than enough of murders. She leant down and patted Jake's soft head, then Leo's. The two dogs were lying quietly together, almost as if they recognised the gravity of the moment.

'Do you know her?' she asked. As one of two local doctors in Berrywick, Sean knew just about everyone in the village, at least by sight.

'No. But it's a fair. She could be from any one of the nearby villages, or even further afield. A tourist, perhaps.'

'I wonder who she is.'

Julia looked at the dead woman and tried to imagine a life for her. It was something she used to do in her job as a social worker and Head of Youth Services. Try to work out what sort of person she was dealing with, right from the start. Their history, long ago and recent. There were always clues.

Did this woman have a husband or children? Parents? A pet? What work did she do? She looked like a down-to-earth sort of person. No make-up, except for a light smear of lipstick. Her hair was cut short in a practical style and tinted a mid-brown. No wedding ring. Plain gold rings in her ears. Neat and tidy, nothing out of place, except for a stain on the side of her grey trousers, as if she'd brushed against something and wiped it off. A stain on her nice clean trousers must have annoyed her, thought Julia. A no-nonsense sort, Julia decided. No frills. She could have worked with Julia, a social worker or an administrator of some sort.

'Oh God, I wonder if someone's waiting for her,' Julia said, thinking of a friend sitting at one of the trestle tables outside the marquee, checking the time on their phone, wondering where she was. Or someone at home, lunch waiting in the warming drawer.

The horrible thought was interrupted by the sound of voices in the maze, and clicks and beeps that Julia recognised as coming from a walkie-talkie.

'They're coming.'

As she said it, a young chap in wellington boots who Julia took to be the groundsman entered the opening Sean and Julia had come through not long before, followed by two police officers. Behind them were two medics with a stretcher. Julia greeted DC Walter Farmer, who was surprised to see her. 'Mrs Bird, are you...?'

'Yes,' she answered.

The female police officer interrupted, addressing Sean. 'Oh hello, Dr O'Connor. Fancy seeing you here. DC Lilian Carson, remember me? The pneumonia, last winter? You prescribed an antibiotic.'

'Hello, Lilian. Yes, of course.' Sean seemed unsure as to whether he should inquire after her health, but decided to let it go, under the circumstances.

'So you found the body?'

'Yes. Mrs Bird and I came upon her in the maze. I checked for pulse and breathing immediately, of course. No sign of life, I'm afraid.'

'Any thoughts on cause of death? In your professional opinion.'

'No sign of foul play, but I didn't move her, of course, so I haven't examined her. I'd say it's likely a stroke or heart attack.'

'Could we back up a bit, sir, and get a full statement?'

Julia took the dogs' leads and moved away, allowing the officials access to the body. DC Farmer bent over the body. He was wearing gloves.

The rather peaceful scene of a woman on a bench was gone, replaced by the busyness of medical bureaucracy. Now it would be transport and autopsies and finding the family. Julia felt saddened by it all.

She watched DC Farmer move the raincoat gently to one side, peering into the basket. He moved it to the other side and then straightened up, addressing his colleague. 'There doesn't seem to be any identification. No purse or handbag that I can see, but I don't want to disturb the evidence. Best to wait until the boss gets here. DI Gibson is on her way, but she's all the way over in Hayfield, following up a lead. She'll be another fifteen or twenty minutes then, I expect.'

Addressing Julia, DC Carson said, 'In the meantime, could I take your statement, ma'am?'

'Of course.'

Julia handed the dogs to Sean and walked over to the young woman, who was standing at the ready, notebook and pen in hand. Julia gave her own statement, the same as Sean's, answered a few questions and provided her contact details. It wasn't much, but the police officer took it all down, and thanked her.

'All right if we go?' Sean asked. Jake was pulling at the leash and even Leo was starting to get bored and restless. As for Julia, she felt quite shaky from the adrenaline.

'Yes, thanks for your time, Doctor. Thanks, ma'am.'

'Er, how do we get out?' Julia asked the groundsman.

'Left at the first four splits, right at the next four and you're home,' he said. He looked at her sternly and added, 'Don't tell anyone.'

'Your secret is safe with me.'

The groundsman's instructions deposited them efficiently at the exit within minutes, demolishing the illusion of endless options of roads less travelled. They hesitated, wondering what to do next. The dogs looked on expectantly.

'Should we go home?' Sean asked. 'I don't think I can face the stalls and shoppers.'

'Let alone the maypole dancing, which is what was on offer at one o'clock, if I remember correctly.'

Sean looked pained at the very idea. The cheerful spring spirit had deserted them. The noise and activity of the Berrywick Spring Fair that had been charming when they arrived, was too much to bear after their sad discovery.

'I know it sounds awful, after the body and everything, but I'm starving,' Julia said. 'Shall we stop by the food stalls and pick something up? We can take it home, eat it on the patio if it's warm enough.'

'That sounds perfect,' Sean said, his face relaxing at the thought. 'Good plan.' He took her hand and they set off in the direction of the fair.

Like many a good plan, this one was foiled in the execution. It was lunchtime, and everyone had had the same idea – let's get us a nice slice of pizza and a beer and sit in the sun. Queues snaked in front of every food truck. The sound of chatter competed with 'Summer of '69'. The dogs were agitated by all the noise, and the humans likewise.

'I've got roasted carrot soup in the freezer – let's just get home,' Julia said, eventually, after several attempts to find a food truck without queues.

'Agreed. Tell you what, let's go past the cake stall and I'll buy a cake for after the soup. It won't be crazy like this, I'm sure.'

The cake stall was quite depleted – good news for the WI – but there were still plenty of cakes to choose from. Including Julia's own, she noted, rather hurt.

'Well, hello,' said Candy. 'And how are the good boys? Having a good fair?'

'Very nice, thanks,' Julia said. She hardly felt she could mention the dead woman. 'Have you been busy?'

'Oh, yes. We did the judging and that was fun. A local chap did it, a sort of celebrity? He has a music show, classical, I think? Always exciting, the judging. It's quite competitive, you know?'

'I'm sure it is,' Julia said. 'Who won? Let me guess, the big green spring wreath?'

Candy rolled her eyes. 'Well, funny you should mention the wreath. Yes, the wreath won. There was a bit of a drama right afterwards. An accident? Well, long story short, the cake fell! Such a mess!'

'Oh, no! It must have been hours of work. All those cupcakes and silver balls and the icing flowers...'

'They were all made by hand, the decorations? Poor Aretha – she's the baker – was in a terrible state. It was an accident, of course, but she blamed Ursula. Ursula is another one of our bakers – she made the pink cake with the white piping?'

Julia shook her head to indicate that she'd not noticed the pink and white cake, but was regretful of the oversight.

'Lovely it was, so pretty and cheerful. One of the first to be bought. Anyway, Ursula was right there when the wreath fell. There was, I don't know, a jostle? People coming past? I don't quite know what happened. Next thing you know, it's slipped off the table onto the ground.'

They both looked at the ground with its telltale crumbs of cake iced with green, and a lone, crushed, edible white blossom.

'How awful.'

'Aretha saw the commotion and came over, and wasn't she furious when she saw her cake on the floor? Can't say I blame her, it was very disappointing, but she's screaming at Ursula, says she knows it was her. That she can't stand losing and had done it on purpose. Ooh, can you imagine?'

'What happened in the end?' Julia was now properly intrigued by the high drama at the cake table. It was refreshingly wholesome and low-stakes compared to the drama of death she'd just been exposed to.

'There was a bit of shouting and Ursula stormed off. She might have gone to clean up? She had been in the path of the cake when it fell. It stains something awful, that food colouring, doesn't it? Anyway, she left, and then Aretha marched off too. Thank goodness. Gosh, wasn't that a scene?'

At that moment, Sean appeared with the dogs' leads in one

hand and a smile on his face. "All good, Julia?" he asked, and then pointed to one of the cakes on the table.

'I'll take this one,' he said to Candy, indicating Delicious Foolproof Chocolate Sponge the Second, and handing her a ten-pound note. His blue eyes gleamed with humour when they met Julia's. 'I fancy this. The best of the lot.'

4

It was pleasant to be home. Sean and Julia sat in companionable silence, hardly speaking, spooning the spicy orange soup rhythmically into their mouths. It might be spring officially, but it had still been too chilly to sit out and they were at the kitchen table. Julia had divided the lone beer in the fridge between two glasses, and they sipped it slowly. The gentle creaking snores of the dogs filled the spaces between their occasional words. Julia's mixed bunch of spring flowers was in a vase on the sideboard. The smell drifted through the room, making Julia feel like she might be in a spring meadow, or perhaps one of those shops that sold ludicrously expensive candles.

Julia finished her food, picked up the napkin from her lap, and dabbed at her mouth. Sean took his last mouthful and reached over to take her plate from her.

'Thank you,' she said. 'Just put them on the side, we can wash up later.'

She took the last sip of her beer, leaned back in her chair, stretched her legs out and tried not to think of the poor woman who was no doubt laid out in the cold morgue at this very moment. When she and Peter had first talked about splitting up, she'd thought about living alone, and her secret horror had been dying in the night and not being found. Well, this woman had been found, at least. Thank goodness she and Sean had decided to walk the maze, and thank goodness Jake had found the centre, or the body might be lying there still.

Sean came back to the table with two plates, each holding a generous slice of chocolate cake and a silver cake fork. He gave one plate to her and sat down with the other on his knee.

Julia cut the tip of her slice with the side of the fork, speared it, and brought it to her mouth. It fell off the fork, bounced down her jumper like a boulder down a mountain, and landed icing-down on her thigh. 'Oh dear,' she said, picking up the bit of cake and popping it into her mouth. She began scraping the icing off her jersey with the fork, looking down at the trousers, which were next in line for a clean-up. 'How annoying. I hope it doesn't leave a stain.' She looked around for a tissue or a cloth.

Candy's story of Aretha and Ursula and the green wreath cake popped into her head. She thought about what Candy had said about the food colouring staining. And then she remembered another stain, another pair of trousers. A smudge. Something greenish.

'Sean!' she said, putting her plate and fork down hard on the side table and getting to her feet. 'I think I know who the dead woman is.'

DI Hayley Gibson's phone had gone straight to voicemail. Julia called the police station and tried to badger the desk sergeant into telling her whether or not Hayley was there, and then putting her through.

'Tell her it's Julia Bird,' she said. 'Tell her it's in connection with a case. She will take my call, I'm sure of it.'

'Hold on a moment, please,' came the reluctant reply. 'I'll see if she is available.'

After a minute of plinky plonky piano music, Hayley's brisk voice came on the line: 'So you found another body, Julia. This must be some sort of record. And honestly, not in a good way.'

'Hello, Hayley. Yes, although to be fair this is hardly the same as the last ones. This one was natural causes, after all.'

Hayley snorted, as if to say that didn't change the fact that Julia had found another body.

'I was wondering. Do you know who she is?' asked Julia.

'No ID on her. We're following some leads, but...'

The way she said it, Hayley's leads didn't sound very promising.

'Well, it might sound a bit odd, but I think I might be able to help with that. When we were at the fair, before the maze, we were at a cake sale – a competition – and I was talking to the woman in charge of the cakes. Candy, her name was, which I thought was rather funny.'

Hayley cut in, 'Julia, do you know who the dead woman is?'

'Yes, I think I do. One of two people, at any rate.'

'Two people? But how...?'

Indistinct voices interrupted Hayley's question. Julia heard her answering impatiently. 'What? Can't you handle it? I'm on a call, for goodness' sake.'

Her voice came back to full volume as she addressed Julia. 'Are you at home?'

'Yes.'

'Sit tight. I have to sort something out here. I'll come past you on my way over to... Never mind. I'll come by.'

She killed the call without waiting for an answer.

'So you think the dead woman is Ursula.' Hayley leaned on her elbows, fixing Julia with her clever blue eyes. The two women were seated across from each other, a tea tray between them. Sean had left before the detective arrived.

'Yes. At least I think it's most likely her. Although it's possible that it's Aretha. She might also have got the green icing on her clothes when the cake fell. But from what Candy said, Ursula took the brunt of it. It's more likely her. But as I said, one of the two.'

'Surnames?' Hayley was abrupt when she was stressed.

'I don't know. Candy would know, though. Or someone else from the WI. Anyone who donated a cake would have filled in a form. I know I did. Let me have a look at the email about the cake sale, there must be a phone number.'

'Okay, do it now. I hate to think of a family sitting and waiting, wondering where she is.'

Hayley tapped her fingers on the table while Julia opened Gmail on her phone and found the email from the WI. There was a contact person.

'Got it. No number for Candy, but the mail came from someone called Gerda, and there's a phone number. Ready?'

Hayley nodded and Julia read out the number to her as she dialled.

'Yes, hello. Is that Gerda? It's Detective Inspector Hayley Gibson here,' Hayley said, Julia watching expectantly. 'I'm trying to locate someone who might be able to shed light on an incident that happened at the Berrywick Spring Fair. Two people, in fact. They both donated cakes to your fundraiser. First names are Aretha and Ursula, could you look up their surnames for me?'

There was a long pause – during which time the person on the other end found the women's details on the forms – and then Julia heard tinny indistinct words coming from the other side. Hayley wedged her mobile between her ear and her shoulder and scribbled in her notebook. 'Ah, yes, Grey with an "e"? Thank you. And Ursula? Benjamin. Thank you. Do you perhaps have contact numbers for them? Wonderful, thank you.' There was more scribbling, nodding and grunting. 'Could you tell me – I know it's an odd question – but do you know what the two women look like? I'm trying to place them.'

The sound of talking leaked from the phone, but Julia couldn't make out a word. The suspense was killing her. She waved to Hayley, pointed to the phone and then to her own ear. She made a 'talking' motion, opening and closing her hand. Hayley frowned in confusion and then it dawned on her – she put the phone on speaker.

'...Aretha is petite with dark hair, long. She usually wears it up in a sort of bun, a chignon I think you call it. Dark eyes. I think her people were from Italy, although they live down Grayton way, I think...'

This was not a description of the dead woman.

Hayley cut in, 'And Ursula Benjamin?'

'I've never met her, so I don't know what she looks like, or anything about her.'

'Do you have an email address for her?'

There was a pause, and Gerda came back on the line. 'Here we are. It's ebenjamin@stmartinschool.co.uk. Ah, so...'

'Right, she works at the school. You've been a big help, thank you.'

Hayley ended the call and stood up. 'If it's one of them, it's Ursula. Aretha looks nothing like our Jane Doe,' she said, putting her phone in her pocket, ready to leave. 'I'd better get back to the station, get some of my people working on this immediately. See if they can positively identify her and find her family.'

'It's her, look,' Julia said, showing Hayley her phone. 'I googled "Ursula Benjamin St Martin" and here she is in the school newsletter.' And sure enough there she was, on Julia's phone screen – the dead woman, but alive, and wearing a tight smile. She had the same neat, low-maintenance haircut and, Julia noticed, seemed to be wearing the same grey jumper.

'"Ursula Benjamin is congratulated on fifteen years of

service to St Martin's. Ursula is a stalwart of the maths department..." And so on.'

Hayley looked slightly abashed. 'Thanks, Julia. Clever of you to notice the green smears. And googling her... Good thinking.'

'Well, you would have done that next.'

'I know I asked you to keep out of police business, but...'

'Of course. You're right. Just happened to have a thought, and I'm passing it on to the authorities, as any good citizen would. I hope you manage to find the family quickly; they must be worried.'

Hayley hesitated and then sat down again. 'I'm going to tell you something, but please, not for public consumption just yet – it is possible that Ursula didn't die of a heart attack or a stroke. It's possible she was killed. The coroner's report hasn't been completed, but we're treating this as suspicious.'

Julia felt like the blood had drained out of her body. She couldn't believe what Hayley was saying – that the poor woman who had died in the maze might have been murdered.

'Oh, goodness,' she murmured. 'How awful.'

'Yes,' said Hayley. 'But not a word, because we're not a hundred per cent sure yet. I really shouldn't be telling you, Julia – but I know that I can count on your discretion.'

'So what happens next?' Julia asked.

'Now that we know who she is, we will get in touch with the family, and see what we can find out in the way of possible people that we need to question. It's seldom that a murder – if that's what it was – is a random act of violence. The killer usually has a reason, however warped. We need to start getting a feel for who Ursula Benjamin was. And who might have wanted to kill her.'

Julia spoke up: 'I think you should talk to Aretha.'

Hayley ran her hands up the sides of her head, making her

short hair spike up. It was a gesture she made quite often, usually when perplexed or exasperated.

'Aretha?' she said in disbelief. 'The other cake lady?'

'Yes. I wasn't there, but from what I heard the altercation between Ursula and Aretha sounded pretty serious. Shouting, arguing, going off in a huff. I know it sounds crazy, but it might have gotten out of hand.'

'Damn right it sounds crazy. Whoever heard of someone killing a person over a WI cake sale?'

Julia shrugged, as if to say that, yes, it was crazy, but they both knew that human nature was varied and unpredictable, and nothing could be discounted.

'Having said that,' Hayley said, in an almost apologetic tone, 'I've seen someone killed over a parking space when I worked up North. And there was once an attempted homicide related to a pear tree – there was an axe involved.'

'Well, those sound every bit as unlikely.'

'I suppose so. I'll get in touch with Aretha Grey when I have the time, but my first priority is to find Ursula's family. Starting with the husband, if there is one.'

5

There were three topics in play at the Buttered Scone. The weather was a perennial favourite, and on this particular Monday, the specific area of meteorological interest amongst the customers was the sudden cold snap. There was general agreement that you shouldn't expect too much of April, which, although technically spring, was not to be trusted and regularly delivered the kind of freezing drizzle that had blown in overnight and was at that very moment knocking against the windows as if it, too, would like to be sitting in the warm tea house, nursing a cup of cocoa, instead of shivering in the high street.

The second topic was crazy old Edna, the old woman who wandered the village, harmlessly muttering to herself and occasionally sharing her garbled wisdom with the villagers. Julia herself had occasionally been on the receiving end of some of Edna's bon mots, so was interested to hear that Edna had, apparently, taken to scavenging through peoples' rubbish – and displaying her finds. Oh, the drama!

'Poor Nina Sommers over in Willow Lane,' said Jane, who Julia knew from book club. 'Edna took out all her empty wine bottles from the trash and lined them up across the road like skittles for bowling. It caused a right little traffic jam until Quentin from across the road moved them all. Poor Nina was too mortified to come out!'

Hilarity greeted this scurrilous tale, but even this fascinating village gossip could not compete with the real news of the day: the death of Ursula Benjamin.

'She was due to retire at the end of this school year, so I hear. So many years of work, the end in sight, and then this. Keels over dead,' said Jane, and gave a shudder, pulling her red Puffa close around her shoulders, as if a sudden chill had come over her.

'My cousin May's next-door neighbour was at the fair when the police and medics brought her out. People said she'd just sat down and died. Do they know what happened to her?' asked Diane, from the next table.

'Must have been an embolism,' said Flo, who, in addition to serving breakfast at the Buttered Scone, was a respected amateur medical expert around these parts. She stopped, a loaded tray in hand, and continued, 'Or possibly a heart attack. It's not been determined, but I dare say we'll know soon enough.'

She took a few more steps to Julia's table and put her plate of scrambled eggs, tomato and bacon in front of her. 'And here's your cappuccino,' she said, handing it to her. Julia took it and thanked her. 'And a biscuit for Jake if he's very good.' Flo looked pointedly at Jake, and put the bone-shaped biscuit on the table, as if she knew there was little hope that he'd reach the required standard of behaviour.

'Ah, thank you, Flo. You're very kind. We are on best behaviour today.'

Julia and Jake usually sat at one of the little outside tables by the door, but a special dispensation had been made in view of the weather, and they were now just inside the door. Julia had explained to Jake in a patient tone, laced with warning, that his best behaviour was expected and a crust of toast would come his way if all went well.

'You're right about the retirement, though, Jane,' said Nicky, who was at the counter waiting for her takeaway coffee. 'Lord knows that after trying to get maths into the thick heads of those naughty kids over at St Martin's, the woman deserved a few good years of gardening and walking. That's what she'd planned, you know. She was going to walk the South West Coast Path, all on her own. She bought fancy new hiking shoes just last week. I saw her round the lanes, breaking them in, she said. But then I heard a rumour that the school persuaded her to stay longer. Something to do with their GCSE results, and offering her a bonus to continue. Poor thing.'

There was general tutting and head shaking. Cups were raised to mouths and lowered to saucers, as the customers of the Buttered Scone contemplated the arbitrariness of life and death.

'You know her then, do you?' Pippa asked. At the sound of her voice, Jake sat up eagerly and wagged his tail. He and his three siblings had lived with Pippa for the first six months of his life, in preparation for their training as guide dogs. The three siblings were on track to be important special needs companions. Jake's temperament was more suited to civilian life, which was why he was now with Julia. He held no grudges against Pippa though, and was always delighted to see her. Pippa, in turn, greeted him with affection now that his lead was in Julia's hand, rather than being tugged out of her own.

'Oh yes,' Nicky answered, over a hiss of steam from the coffee machine. 'Her younger sister and my mum's cousin, Tammy, were friends at uni, and the families used to go camping together when I was a teen. And she helped me with extra lessons when I was at school. Goodness, but she was determined when it came to maths. She didn't let up until she got it into your head. Even managed to get it into mine!' Nicky laughed, knocking her knuckles on her forehead.

'Scared it into you, most likely,' said Jane, and then blushed and stammered, 'not to speak ill of the dead.'

Nicky didn't seem to notice. As usual, once she'd started a story, any small interruptions were swept aside in its wake. 'She moved to Edgely to be closer to the school. After that we didn't see much of her and Robert – that's her husband.'

This was one of the many surprising things Julia had discovered about village life. Edgely was about five miles away, but if someone moved there, it was as if they'd gone to live in Melbourne.

'Poor fellow, it'll be a shock,' said Flo. 'Did they have children?'

'Just the one. Luke. He must be twenty by now, maybe even older. Haven't seen him in years. He might have moved away – in fact, I think he did. Poor lamb, losing his mum like that, so sudden.'

Flo handed Nicky a steaming cup of coffee and foam.

'Thanks, love. Can you put it on my tab?' Nicky said, and moved smoothly back to her topic. 'Anyway, with the upcoming retirement and her walking and so on, she came over this way and I saw her on the paths a bit in the last few weeks. We chatted. She was very happy to be getting out of teaching. The stress, you know. The kids are bad enough, but those parents! Things have changed, is what she said. So sad she didn't live to have her retirement, you know? Perhaps the rumour was true, and they persuaded her to stay longer, and *that's* what gave her the stress and heart attack! Gosh, is that the time? Well, I'll better be off then. It'll be time to fetch Sebastian from nursery in a minute and I haven't even bought anything for his lunch.'

Julia had things to do, too. She polished off the last of her breakfast, saving a crust of toast for Jake as well as his special biscuit, drained the last sip of coffee and waved to Flo for her bill.

The rain had stopped, at least. Although it was definitely hanging about for another go-round. Best to get home before it came down again. Julia set off briskly, Jake trotting happily beside her, and made it home before the next squall.

Julia was fairly certain Hayley would have found out about the husband by now, but she called her just in case. The phone rang and rang and she was just about to ring off when the detective answered.

'Hello, Julia.'

'Hi. Just wanted to let you know that I was down at the Buttered Scone, and I found out about Ursula's husband. You've probably located him, but just in case. His name's Robert. He's an accountant.'

'Thanks. My people tracked him down this morning. He was in London for the week, apparently. That's why nobody had noticed her missing. He's coming back to Berrywick today to ID the body. Just a formality though; it's definitely her.'

'Yes, that's the word at the Buttered Scone.'

'I'm wondering whether we should close the whole intelligence department and just have someone hang around the Buttered Scone for local intel. What else did you hear about her?'

'She's a maths teacher, which we knew, and she was due to retire soon, or perhaps not. It seems a bit unclear. She liked hiking. Not much that's of use, I'm afraid.'

'And what about the husband, and their relationship? I don't suppose he is a renowned philanderer with a fiery temper? That would make my life a bit easier.'

The joke came out more harshly than Hayley might have

intended, and there was a moment of awkward silence before Julia answered.

'No. Nothing like that. Or at least not to the knowledge of the regulars at the Buttered Scone.'

'Well it seems he was out of town at the time, anyway. There was a big match on, apparently. Rugby. We'll check out his alibi if it comes to it, but that's his story.'

'So, you're sure it was...' Julia baulked at the word 'murder', and instead said, 'intentional?'

'Oh, it was intentional, all right. She was definitely murdered. Coroner isn't quite done, but he phoned the boss with his preliminary thoughts. Strangled. Anyway, I have to go. Thanks for the info. If you hear anything else, give me a shout.'

Julia was always slightly taken aback by the way Hayley could deliver some shocking piece of news and then move right on to the next thought. For Julia, it took a bit longer to process. 'Sure,' she told Hayley. 'Quick thing, though, about Aretha...'

'Who?'

'The cake sale lady.'

'Right. Her.' Hayley sounded impatient, even a tad irritated. 'My priority is the husband right now. See what we get from him and follow any leads. The cake sale lady will have to wait.'

6

Julia planned to spend the morning gardening. Spring was a busy time, according to her gardening calendar. This morning, fortified by a good breakfast, she was going to plant seeds in trays, ready to transplant when the weather was warmer. But she had no sooner got her gardening gloves and trowel than the rain started again. Ten minutes later, it was still at it. It looked as if it had settled in.

There would be no gardening today. She mentally surveyed the other tasks and chores on her agenda. There was no point in doing the washing or cleaning the sitting room windows. She couldn't freshen the hens' nesting boxes with new hay. All outdoor tasks were off the table, which left the dreaded admin. Julia groaned and went to fetch her laptop.

She put it on the kitchen table, which doubled as her desk, and opened her mail. Amongst the newsletters and spam and bills there was, at least, an email from Jess in Hong Kong. Julia opened it first, and with anticipation. Jess's emails tended to be polite and remote and thin on personal information, but Julia always hoped for some nugget of gossip or insight, a funny story, the mention of a friend or even, maybe, a lover. This one was chattier than usual, and included the fact that while writing up her master's thesis, Jess might spend some time in England. *I have never even met Dad's Christopher or your Jake, and I guess it's time to check out your new abode in the countryside,* she said.

What happy news! Julia felt a thrill at the possibility, and immediately began drafting a response. The email was too gushy, she thought – she didn't want to scare Jess off – and so she deleted a few exclamation marks and adjectives. Now it sounded rather cold. She added 'you' to the 'love' in the sign-off, but it seemed too much. She added 'to' and deleted that. Why were 'love' and 'love you' and 'love to you' so different? She wished she had easier communication with her only child. She saved the draft and went to make a cup of tea. She'd come back to it later with a fresh eye.

While she waited for the kettle to boil, Julia gazed at the steady drizzle that had scuppered her gardening plans. It was almost hypnotic, the thin grey rain, drops gathering on the windowpane, collecting into a larger drop, and racing down to the sill. Her mind went back to Ursula, and she wondered if Hayley had interviewed the husband yet. Robert. Poor man: imagine going off to watch the rugby and coming home to identify your spouse's body in the morgue.

The click of the kettle brought her back to the present.

She made her tea and took the mug back to the table. The smell of Earl Grey tea mixed with the scent of the flowers she'd bought at the fair was intense. She returned to her laptop and opened a new tab.

Aretha Grey.

Her fingers typed the words almost before her brain had thought them. She hit return, and let Google do its work.

Aretha's spectacular cake was no one-off, it seemed. She owned a little home-bake shop over in Edgely – Ursula's home town too, Julia noted. The web page for Country Treats & Eats promised, 'Jams and preserves, baked goods, frozen meals and very special cakes for special occasions. Made with love from local produce!'

There was a photograph of a rather glamorous woman, her dark hair swept up on her head. Her wine-coloured lips were arranged in a broad smile and she was holding a magnificent confection – a cupcake wreath not unlike the one Julia had seen at the fair, but Christmas themed, with red baubles and silver stars.

Julia closed her laptop. 'Come on Jake,' she said to the dozing dog. 'We're going out to buy jam.'

By the time they got to Edgely, the rain had cleared. Julia found the shop easily, and there was even a parking space in front of it. Jake was in his customary position – sitting upright in the back seat on the passenger side, gazing out of the window like visiting royalty. Julia rolled the windows down a couple of inches and told him to stay. 'I won't be long,' she said. 'Be a good boy and we'll have a walk when I'm finished. Try somewhere new.'

It had occurred to her on the way over that Aretha might not be in the shop, that there might be a manager or sales assistant in charge. So she was pleased to see the woman she recognised from the shop's website behind the counter, wearing the same dark chignon and the same wine-coloured lipstick, helping the only other customer, an older gentleman, with a few packets of shortbread and biscuits.

Julia took a basket and browsed the preserves, settling on raspberry jam and a clementine marmalade. Her own jam-making efforts had been less than successful, and after the messy incident with Jake and the sticky spilled sugar syrup, she'd sworn off the process altogether. From the corner of her eye she watched Aretha handing the old chap his change.

'There you go, Mr Robinson, enjoy your tea.'

'Oh, I will. You know me and those lemon creams.'

'Treat yourself. You deserve it,' she said, patting his arm.

The bell on the door was still jingling from his exit when Aretha asked from behind the counter, 'Hello, is there anything I can help you with?'

'So many delicious things, just making up my mind,' Julia said cheerfully, turning towards her and looking at Aretha as if she was just noticing her. 'Gosh, don't I recognise you from somewhere? I'm sure I saw you somewhere recently?' She made a bit of a show of 'A Person Wracking Her Brains For Errant Information' and then said, in her best tone of sudden realisation, 'Oh, I know where it was! I saw you at the Berrywick Spring Fair, if I'm not mistaken. That's right, you had that marvellous cake, a sort of wreath, wasn't it? With an Easter theme?'

'Ah, yes. That was me.' Aretha smiled.

'It was a beauty. My chocolate sponge was the ugly stepsister by comparison.'

Aretha leaned her forearms on the counter, bent towards Julia and said sternly, 'Now don't you be so hard on yourself. I'm sure it was delicious, and it was for charity, that's the main thing.'

'True,' Julia said, adding a tray of Lamingtons to her basket. 'Ooh, I can't resist these and one so seldom gets them. Now tell me. Did you make all the decorations yourself? The flowers and so on?'

'Yes, all handmade.' Aretha gave a proud little smile, which faded quickly.

'Gosh, how clever. It must have taken ages! I hope you won the competition. It'll be a great injustice if you didn't.'

Aretha rolled her eyes to the ceiling and gave a loud sigh. 'I did. But unfortunately, my cake came to a sticky end – literally. Someone knocked it off the table.'

'What?' Julia hoped that her feigned surprise sounded

genuine. 'I can't believe it! What awful luck! And after all that work. I'm so sorry,' Julia said, and she really was. Poor Aretha looked quite distraught. Julia felt bad about her duplicitousness, but it was for a greater good, she told herself. She wanted to see whether Aretha was a likely suspect or not. 'You must have been so upset. I'd have been furious.'

'Yes, well, I was. Upset and furious. But there's nothing to be done.'

'The person who did it must have felt just awful, too. Imagine, knocking that beauty off the table.'

'I don't know. I think it might have been on purpose,' said Aretha, shrugging. 'You've no idea how horribly competitive some people can be. But anyhow, enough of that. I don't want to speak ill of someone no longer here to defend herself.'

'Wait – are you talking about Ursula Benjamin?'

Aretha straightened up, stammering, 'How do you know? And who do you say you are?'

'I know Ursula died that day at the fair, so I assumed it must be her.'

'I shouldn't have said anything.' Aretha looked horrified at herself, having inadvertently spoken ill of the dead.

'You didn't, I just put two and two together. Don't feel bad.'

'Well, if you know Ursula, you'll know that she could be rather... let's say tricky. She had to have her way, be the best. Not that I'd wish...'

'Of course not.'

'I feel bad about it though. We had a bit of a shouting match. It's my Italian blood. I get worked up. I can't help but wonder if I contributed in some way to, you know... The heart attack. That's what they say she died of.'

'I don't think that's likely. Mostly that sort of thing is genetic, or, you know, lifestyle. It isn't brought on by a row.'

'You're right, I suppose,' Aretha said, looking somewhat

comforted. 'But still, I said some horrible things. They might have been the last words spoken to her, imagine that.'

'You weren't to know she was going to die,' boomed a voice from the door. 'And it's true, she wasn't an easy woman.'

Aretha and Julia both turned in surprise to the source of the voice. It was a strongly-built blonde woman in riding jodhpurs and a big ragged-looking navy jumper. The old chap must have left the door open, because it hadn't rung when she came in.

'Emily!' Aretha said, flustered. 'I didn't hear you come in.'

'Don't look so worried. It's not as if you gave her a heart attack. And let's face it, she was a proper know-all, was our Ursula. Donna had to dissolve her book club to get rid of her, remember? She wouldn't stop telling everyone what was wrong with the books, or their opinions of them.'

'Well, she did have some strong views, I suppose.'

'I'll say. And competitive, too. A friend of mine played tennis with her back at uni, and she said she cheated on the baseline calls.' From the look on Emily's face and her tone of outrage, this was about as bad behaviour as one could imagine of a person.

'Emily, have some decency. The woman died yesterday!' said Aretha.

'I know. And I'm sorry. I actually quite liked her, myself. She was clever. But let's not pretend she wasn't a difficult person, just because she's dead. Now, let's see what you have in the freezer there. I honestly can't bear the thought of making supper again. Every bloody night, isn't it? Forever. Relentless. I mean, what kind of a system is that?' And with that she strode past them to rummage through the home-cooked ready meals.

Julia lifted her basket onto the counter. 'I'm sorry about your cake, and about Ursula. It's horrible for you,' she said, feeling genuine sympathy for Aretha. 'But please don't feel bad, it's not your fault.'

Aretha lifted the raspberry jam to the scanner. 'Thanks,

that's kind of you to say.' She opened up a paper bag and popped the jam in, then reached for the marmalade. 'I suppose that's life, isn't it?' She put the marmalade in the bag and picked up the Lamingtons. 'You just never know what's going to happen, or when it's going to end.'

7

Julia was done with poking her nose into police matters. Her long career in social work had simply reinforced a personality trait she'd had since childhood. Her mother had noted it, as had her teachers, and, later, her ex-husband – Julia found it almost impossible to resist interfering, or helping, if one were to choose a kinder term.

Well, she wasn't a social worker any more. She just had to get used to the fact that it wasn't her job to solve every problem. Jam and cake, that was her remit now.

Anyhow, she'd had her suspicions about Aretha, and she'd been wrong. The visit to Edgely had convinced Julia that there was no way Aretha was Ursula's killer. Luckily Hayley hadn't taken Julia's hunch seriously and treated her as a serious suspect. Julia felt an anxious flush on her skin and her heart beat faster in her chest as she imagined what could have happened. It brought back to her another time when she'd still been working and she'd been wrong – so terribly wrong – about a case.

Now, Julia would back off the investigation, and let the police take care of things.

She had plenty to keep her occupied. Tuesday was spent in the garden doing the jobs she'd planned for Monday – tidying and trimming, and planting vegetable seeds in trays. She took Jake for a long walk on the riverside path.

On her return she found Edna standing outside her house, staring intently at her rubbish bins. 'Can I help you, Edna?' she asked.

'The winds of change blow rubbish,' said Edna, conversationally.

Julia sighed. She didn't feel like she had the energy for this today.

'I'm sure they do, Edna,' she said. 'But if you could refrain from going through my bins, I'd be most grateful.'

'Cometh the hour, cometh the binman,' said Edna, happily. With that, she turned and continued down the road.

Julia took Jake back in, fed him, and made a batch of bolognaise for the freezer. She even had time to read her book – an entertaining read about a woman of her own age who had moved to a charming village in Italy and, most improbably, found herself solving local crimes.

It was a full and pleasant day. Yes, from time to time she wondered about the investigation, whether the coroner's report was in, what Ursula's husband was like, if there had been any leads or tip-offs. But she didn't dwell, or form opinions, and she didn't contact Hayley.

On Wednesday, Julia woke up early to feed the fowl and walk the dog. She always took him on a quick circuit around the neighbourhood before she left for her shift at Second Chances. She harboured the fond hope that the walk would take the edge off Jake's energy, and prevent Wanton Acts of Destruction in her absence. To be on the safe side after the walk, she put the garden hose and fittings up on the patio table, out of reach, and scanned the area for shoes, tools and other chewables. Then she set off.

Wilma had already opened up the shop. As always, she looked as if she'd recently returned from Pilates, or was about to take off on a run. That was to say, fresh-faced, healthy, mildly superior, and wearing a great deal of Lycra. Wilma owned a wide array of stretchy items that could be layered over each other and thus worn for exercise, lounging about, or – as was the case – managing the local charity shop. She accessorised successfully with statement beads and scarves. Julia admired the way Wilma could put everything together and look appropriately and stylishly dressed. She knew that if she tried the same she would look as if she'd come to work in her pyjamas, rather surprisingly over-accessorised.

Diane arrived minutes after Julia, looking a little puffed. Julia saw her walking fast down the road, her shiny ponytail swishing energetically from side to side, flashes of red gold appearing briefly at her shoulders. She was clearly aiming to arrive at the shop on the dot of ten, the official opening time.

'Hello, ladies, lovely day,' she offered, swinging her bag off her arm and onto the counter. Wilma took a surreptitious look at her watch, which wasn't really surreptitious, because both Julia and Diane noticed it. Diane gave Julia a grin and continued her cheerful chatter. 'They say it might rain. It certainly doesn't look like it.'

They all looked outside, and up at the sky, as if to confirm her opinion.

'Still, you never know. What's the plan for today, Wilma?'

The plan was fairly standard. Sorting donations, pricing and marking them, tidying the shop, keeping the displays fresh. Nonetheless, Wilma ran through the tasks for the day: 'The spring-themed window display still looks good, it has only been in a couple of weeks, but you could go and check that it's all in order – I noticed one of the fluffy bunnies had fallen over.

There might be a bit of dust to get rid of. And we got three boxes of books that came in yesterday. They'll need going through. Julia, do you want to do that?'

'Happy to.' It was true, Julia rather enjoyed rifling through the boxes of books, sorting them into more and less sellable, pricing them accordingly, and writing the prices in pencil inside the covers.

They agreed on a preparatory cup of tea before they got into their tasks, and moved into the storeroom that doubled as a back office, and which held a tiny tea station – a kettle, a few mugs, jars of tea bags and sugar all laid out on top of a tiny fridge where they kept milk and cold water, and sometimes lunches brought from home. Just as they'd poured the cups and decided against the biscuits – 'Too close to breakfast, let's wait a bit' – Diane's phone rang.

'It's my mum. Better take it,' she said, touching the screen and putting it to her ear.

Julia zoned out. As she sipped her tea, she began to draw up a shopping list in her head. She would pick up a few things when she left Second Chances.

Butter
Spaghetti
White onions
Washing up liquid

Diane's voice began to encroach on her consciousness.

'I know, I heard. I didn't know her, but isn't it so sad? And so sudden. One minute she's enjoying a day out, the next... Hmmm. What? Oh no, Mum, nothing like that. I think you're mistaken... Really? Are you sure...? Oh, see. She heard that herself, did she? Not just gossip...? I didn't mean... Well I never, who'd have thought...? Yes, that's true, you never can tell... Mum, I have to go, I'm at the shop. I'll pop by on my way home, we can chat then.' She lowered the phone and said in a dramatic tone, 'Well I never!'

'What?' Wilma asked.

'The woman who died at the fair? Ursula someone? It looks like it wasn't a heart attack. Seems the police think she was killed. Mum's friend works with a lady whose husband is the maintenance chap at the school where the dead lady worked. Said the police had been there, taking statements.'

Julia tried to compose her face into an expression of mild surprise, not wanting to let on that she had found the body, or that the news of the circumstances of Ursula's death was not new information to her. 'Did they say how she died?' she asked.

'They say she was strangled,' Diane said, almost whispering the last word.

Strangled. It was a brutal word indeed, with its tangled, guttural letters following the hissing S.

'Good heavens, but how...?' Wilma started, and then stopped talking at the ring of the bell on the front door.

'I'll go,' said Julia, eager to move. She walked through to the shop and came face to face with a tall grey-haired man struggling through the door with a bulging bin bag held between his arms.

'We would like to make a donation,' he said in a clipped tone, setting the bag down on the floor. 'Of clothes, women's clothes.'

A younger man followed him with an equally voluminous bag, which he dropped at Julia's feet as if he couldn't wait to get rid of it. 'Here's some more,' he said gruffly. 'There's a box of stuff in the car, I'll go and get it.' He turned and left, leaving Julia with the older man who, she realised, must be the father of the younger. The youngster's hair was golden and his eyes blue, while the father's colouring was darker, but they had the same lanky body, the same large narrow nose and deep-set eyes.

'Thank you,' said Julia. 'That's very much appreciated. As you know, it all goes to a good cause.'

The first thing Wilma had told Julia when she started working at the shop was not to ask where any donations came from. Too often, the answer entailed death, divorce, or downsizing to a little retirement place somewhere. Depressing, distressing or disheartening.

Diane came through from the back room. 'Let me give you a hand with that,' she said, reaching for the nearest bag, and hauling it back from where she'd come.

The youngster came back straining to carry a heavy box.

'Just pop it down there, thank you,' said Julia, indicating the counter and then reaching under it for the clipboard and form. 'If I could just get your details, please.'

'No need,' the older man said, waving it away. 'You're welcome to it all. We have to go.'

'It's a requirement, I'm afraid. Just in case. It won't take a moment.'

'In case of what?' asked the youngster, tetchily.

'A formality, really, but you never know. We might find something personal you've popped in by mistake. And we like to have a record, in case something turns out to be stolen. Not that...'

'It's not *stolen*,' the youngster said. 'Who would steal a bunch of old clothes? Old woman's clothes and books? We just want to get rid of it, is all. We just want it out of the house. Couldn't look at it. Can't bear to... Isn't that what you...?'

'Luke,' the father said, his warning tone softened with kindness.

'Of course, I completely understand,' said Julia, keeping her tone light and polite. 'It will just take a minute.'

'Just take the stuff!'

'Why don't you wait in the car, Luke? I'll fill this in and be out in a minute.'

Luke hesitated a moment, nodded grimly at his father, and slouched out of the shop.

'Sorry about that, he's had a hard couple of days. He's been living in New Zealand, just got back, and then... Anyway, what do you need from me?'

'Just the basics: name, address, phone number...' Julia said, taking up the clipboard and pen.

The man sighed. 'The name's Robert Benjamin,' he said

Julia looked up and before she knew it, the word 'Oh!' slipped out. And then, 'I'm sorry.'

Whether she was sorry for his wife's death, or her outburst, or the form-filling, she wasn't sure. All of it, most likely. She stood there awkwardly for a moment, her pen poised above the clipboard.

'Robert Benjamin,' she repeated, keeping her voice steady. She wrote it down. He gave her his phone number and his address in Edgely. Julia wrote them down.

She cleared her throat ahead of the final question, and looked at him with what she hoped was gentleness, 'Source of items?'

'They are my wife's clothes. She is deceased,' he said, formally.

'Ursula Benjamin,' she said. 'I'm sorry for your loss.'

'Thank you. Did you know her?' he asked.

'No.' The answer was truthful, as the question was asked, but it didn't provide a complete account of their acquaintance. Julia didn't know whether or not to mention that she was the one who'd found his wife. She hesitated a moment too long, and just as she opened her mouth to tell him, Robert said, 'Well, thank you for your help. I'd better get back to my son. As you can imagine, it's not an easy time.'

'Of course. Awful. He must be absolutely devastated.'

He just shook his head sadly, no words, and left the shop.

8

'Tolstoy,' yelled the man in the blue raincoat, setting out after his dog at a furious stomp. 'Come back here, Tolstoy.'

Sean and Julia shared a look. 'That's a good one for the list,' she said. 'I wonder if he regrets it?'

'Doubtless.'

'But perhaps not as much as the owner of Mr Bow Wow.'

They had a mental list of amusing dog names, entries garnered from their long walks with the sensibly-named Leo and Jake. It was one of the nice things about being in a relationship, Julia thought – shared amusements and familiar jokes.

'Poor woman, shouting that all over the park. Still, she could just use Bow or Mister, for calling purposes.'

'Not Mister. People would think she was calling an errant husband. "You get back here, Mister!"'

Sean laughed at that and took her hand, their arms swinging slightly between them as they walked. The park showed signs of spring – the daffodils were out – but the air cooled quickly as the sun headed towards the horizon, and Julia was glad of her jacket. The dogs ran ahead, off lead, chasing each other across the flower-strewn grassy field in the direction of the lake.

'Tell me about your day, Mister,' she said.

'Just a regular day in the surgery, nothing much to report there. Lots of seasonal allergies, this time of year. The usual array of illnesses and injuries. I sent one chap for an X-ray, I think his twisted ankle might be a fracture.'

'I must say, I thought doctoring would be a bit more exciting. Based on television series, entirely.'

'You don't want exciting in my line of work.'

'Nor in mine, believe me.' Julia shuddered in a visceral recollection of the feeling of utter horror and despair that she'd experienced with some of the really bad cases she'd worked on. Their arms had stopped their carefree swinging and Sean squeezed her hand in response to the sudden tension in her body.

'Ah, Julia. I don't know how you dealt with all those troubled youths. That's the worst, for me. Teens with problems. Depression, that sort of thing. It's so sad.'

'It is really hard and painful, seeing them struggling to cope. I suppose I got rather used to it, and I took some comfort from knowing that they were getting help. I felt I could be useful to them and their families.' It struck her that she missed it, being useful. That was why she was working in Second Chances, and interfering in matters that weren't her business. Like the death of Ursula Benjamin.

'It's true, I also feel better when I can help,' Sean said. 'But it's not always easy. Sometimes you can't hand out an antibiotic or stitch up a cut. Sometimes... I don't know... Last week I had a girl with an eating disorder, and a boy who was using black market steroids. One trying to get smaller and thinner and one trying to get bigger and bulkier. Made me wonder about the world they inhabit.'

'It's very sad. I came across quite a bit of that in my work. The eating disorders seem more prevalent than ever. The steroids are quite a new thing. There seems to be a wave amongst the young men and even teenage boys.'

Sean looked quite stricken at the thought, and said, 'Not something I'd have expected in our little village. The world's changing, I suppose. Even in Berrywick.'

Now it was Julia's turn to give him a comforting squeeze of the hand. He turned to her with a small smile, and pulled himself from his gloom.

'So that was my day, just your basic medical problems. I left a bit early because I had to go into the police station this afternoon and give an official statement about Ursula's death. The latest information on that is that she was definitely strangled. The police told me that they believe someone came up behind her.'

'Isn't it awful. And odd, too, isn't it? We didn't notice any marks.'

'The polo neck of her jersey would have protected the skin somewhat from grazes from a rope, if that's what was used. And remember we didn't move anything, so we couldn't see much of her neck. I might have seen something if I'd given her a proper examination, but even then, sometimes there are no external marks.'

'Where's the rope? We didn't see anything lying around.'

'I asked the same of the police. They said that they did a proper search and there was nothing on the scene. No rope or anything like it – a belt, the strap of a handbag. He likely took whatever it was with him when he left. There were some footprints which might have been made by the killer, but from what I understood, they weren't sure if they could get clear enough moulds to be very useful.'

In the distance, she saw the dogs loop back and run towards them. They were well matched in terms of speed – Jake had the advantage of youth, but was a clumsy fellow; Leo was older and slower, but much nippier round the corners and less distractible.

Keeping an eye on the dogs, Julia told Sean about Robert and Luke's donation.

'That's very quick, isn't it?' he said. 'She hasn't been dead a week.' He sounded properly shocked.

'I also thought it was a bit strange, but the lad said they couldn't stand the sight of the clothes, wanted them out of the house. He'd obviously arrived back for the memorial and they'd got cracking. One thing I've learned in my work is that people process grief in very different ways. Some people hang on to mementos and can't let go; they're often the ones who take forever to resolve the practical issues around the death. Others want to get the personal effects dealt with and the paperwork done and dusted before the body's even cold. There's no right or wrong.'

'Of course,' Sean said. 'Wise woman, you are. You should be a social worker.'

'I'm ready for a change, actually. Although the dog rearing and chicken farming isn't nearly as lucrative as I'd anticipated.'

They laughed.

The dogs arrived at speed. The humans instinctively braced themselves and softened their knees to lessen the chance of injury in case of impact, but Jake lumbered by, just brushing against Julia with his tail, and Leo missed them both. They galloped off in the direction of the lake.

'What was the husband like?' Sean asked Julia, as if they hadn't been interrupted.

'Reserved. Almost formal. I couldn't read him, really. The son was more emotional, quite stirred up, even angry. Robert was kind and calm with him, he tried to contain his son's emotion. What did Hayley say? Is the husband a suspect?'

'I doubt Hayley would tell me if he was,' Sean said. 'As we know, the spouse or lover is always first in line for suspicion, and she did interview him of course. I happened to overhear one of the officers say that they had someone checking whether the husband had been in London, as he claimed, when the murder happened.'

'Well, if he was in London and it wasn't the cake lady, I wonder who it might be?'

'What cake lady? What are you talking about?'

'Oh nothing, just a hunch I had that was completely wrong.'

He did that quizzical raised eyebrow thing that made him look even more like Sean Connery than he usually did, and gave her a knowing smile. 'I thought you were done with your amateur sleuthing.'

'You thought correctly. I am. No sleuthing. Let's get those dogs back, shall we? Before they decide on a swim.'

Sean's ear-splitting whistle stopped the dogs in their tracks and brought them hurtling back, tongues and tails waving merrily.

A message from DC Walter Farmer awaited Julia when she checked her phone on her return home from the walk. Could she please bring the shoes she was wearing when she found the body, so as to eliminate her footprints from those found at the scene? It was 6 p.m. already and she had to get the hens settled and feed Jake before she even thought of supper for herself. She felt sure Walter could wait until tomorrow. She replied with a message that she'd be in at ten the next morning.

With the animals fed, Julia made herself a ham and cheese toasted sandwich – promising that tomorrow she'd make a salad or something equally virtuous to make up for tonight's high-carb-zero-veg laziness. It was delicious, if not terribly nutritious, and she ate it in minutes, washed down with a glass of the fresh pressed apple juice made and bottled by a local farmer.

Her task for the evening was to write back to Jess about her possible visit. She felt bad about having overthought and finally abandoned her response, instead of writing back immediately and enthusiastically. Julia noted that she and Jess had the inverse of many mother-daughter relationships. They had sailed breezily through the usually difficult teenage years without any fuss, but as Jess had reached young adulthood, when a bit more independence and distance often made things less fraught, they'd got scratchier and found it more difficult to connect. And then Julia and Peter's marital break-up had sent Jess dashing off to study in Hong Kong to avoid the fallout. It seemed that now she was edging back.

Julia couldn't do anything about the tardiness of her response, but she could write back with genuine enthusiasm, and an open heart. She wrote what she felt.

> *I am thrilled that you plan to visit. I have a lovely spare room all set up and ready for you. I know Dad is eager for you to meet Christopher and vice versa. Jake is a very friendly and enthusiastic chap and, I can assure you, will be delighted to make your acquaintance. Probably too delighted – you may have to fend him off.*
>
> *I should probably tell you that you will meet another special chap, assuming things continue on their current path. I've been 'seeing someone', a kind and clever man called Sean, the village doctor. Believe me, I am probably as surprised as you are by this turn of events. The very last thing on my mind was a new relationship. Anyhow, I think the two of you will get on well. He is very direct, and quick with a laugh. Also, he looks like Sean Connery – the best of the Jameses, as we always agreed!*
>
> *The biggest surprise of all, I suspect, will be your mum. I do feel I've changed, profoundly, in the past year. It's to be expected – ending a marriage and moving away are on anyone's list of big life changes and stressful situations.*

Although, I've found this new time of my life strangely suitable and invigorating.

Only now that I've retired do I realise how utterly absorbed I was in my work, and how emotionally taxing it was. I believe that our relationship suffered as a result, and for that I'm truly, deeply sorry.

Darling girl, do let me know the likely timing of your visit as soon as you can. I miss you and am so looking forward to seeing you, to showing you my new life and hearing all about yours.

Love

Mum

Before she could read it and second guess herself, tone down her enthusiasm or hit delete on some of her revelations and admissions, she pressed send.

9

DC Walter Farmer took Julia's shoes from her and put them in a clear plastic bag with *Evidence Bag* printed on it, and a complicated tamper-proof ziplock sort of closing mechanism. Her brown walking shoes looked rather scuffed and sad, lying there in this very smart, very official bag. They were fairly new and she had always thought of them as smart and serviceable when they were on her feet.

'We'll have them back to you in a few days, I expect,' the young policeman said. 'Thank you, ma'am.'

'You're welcome, Walter. Anything I can do to help.'

He hesitated a moment, the bag dangling from his hand, then asked, 'Do you know Mr Benjamin at all, Mrs Bird?'

'Robert Benjamin?'

'Yes.'

'No. He and his son Luke came into Second Chances when I was working there yesterday, but that's the first time I'd ever met them.'

'Did Mr Benjamin look familiar at all, to you? You didn't see him at the fair, maybe?'

'I don't think I've ever seen him before, but I'm not sure I would have recognised him from the fair. There were a lot of people there. Anyway, wasn't he in London?'

Walter nodded in a resigned sort of way. 'Yes. So he says. And his story does seem to check out. He has a witness to corroborate his story that he was at a rugby match in London. He even had the train ticket home, London to Gloucester, the day after Ursula died. It's in evidence. It's just... I don't know. I feel there's something off about him. He had a sort of nervous manner. Like maybe he's hiding something.'

'I wouldn't know about that, Walter. His wife has just died; that would throw anyone into a strange state. He seemed quite normal to me, although he was only in the shop a few minutes, dropping off Ursula's clothes and some personal things. He was reserved, businesslike about the whole process. Poor Luke was quite worked up, though. Hard for him.'

'Poor fellow. His dad said he flew home as soon as he heard about his mum's death, of course. Imagine coming back all that way from New Zealand on the plane, knowing you're going to bury your dead mum.'

'Awful. It's about twenty-four hours, I think. Even more, depending on how you travel. Just unimaginable, sitting there in that uncomfortable aeroplane seat, or in some layover in who-knows-where, and thinking...' Julia couldn't help imagining Jess in the same situation, travelling from Hong Kong. Her eyes started to fill up with tears.

'And then having to clear out all her clothes. My mum and I did that when Dad died. Awful, it was.'

This was the first time Walter had shared anything personal with Julia. She had no idea about his mum or dad, whether he had a boyfriend or girlfriend, if he lived alone or with family or friends. He'd always just been DI Hayley Gibson's rather inconspicuous sidekick. Julia felt bad about her inattention – although to be fair, when she saw DC Walter Farmer there were usually more pressing matters than small talk at hand. Like dead bodies.

'I'm sorry, Walter. It's so hard, losing your dad. And the clearing out of personal things is very difficult and sad.'

'We didn't do it so soon, though. We waited a few months. I couldn't have done it earlier.'

'Well, the poor chap said he couldn't stand to see all his mum's things in the house. Each to their own, I suppose.'

'Well, I hope we can find out what happened to her. And I hope it's not... I mean, it would be even more awful for Luke if...' Walter stopped himself from finishing the sentence.

There was a pause while they considered the unsaid second half of the sentence, which was, of course, 'if it turns out his dad killed her.'

Walter looked very young, his brow furrowed in concern, his chin still struggling under a light rash of the last teenage pimples. He straightened up to his not inconsiderable and distinctly gangly height, and said in a professional tone, 'I'd better get back to work, Mrs Bird. Thank you for bringing these in. I'll get them back to you as soon as I can.'

The high street was quite abustle. The tourists had arrived with the spring and the swallows. In a month or two, when summer and school holidays coincided, residents would be jostling their way through the crowds of ice-cream eaters and bird-spotters and river-walkers and pub-crawlers and waterpark-seekers. For now, the visitors were around in significant but not excessive numbers, most of them close to Julia's age and clad in sensible outerwear and good walking shoes.

A couple of them were blocking the pavement while looking in the window of the travel agent. 'Greece might be nice for next year,' the solid, grey-haired woman was saying to her slightly younger companion. 'Or Turkey.'

'I hear Turkey's lovely, and I've never been. But I was thinking of South Africa. We could do a safari and then the coast.'

Julia found it amusing that the two women would be spending their current holiday discussing their next holiday. It was the exact opposite of the 'be in the moment' mantra that was meant to apply to travel.

As for herself, her real life still felt rather like a holiday. She wondered when she'd go abroad again, and where. Perhaps to Hong Kong, she thought. If Jess came to England this year, maybe Julia could visit her next. She felt a little rush of pleasure at the thought and, on a whim, pushed open the door of the travel agent and went inside.

'How can I help you plan your dream trip?' The question came from a young woman at a desk tucked away to the right of the door. Both girl and desk were dwarfed by a huge poster of a white beach and blue water, the sun beating relentlessly down on the scene. The woman, whose name tag said *Sandi*, looked as if she could use an afternoon on a sunlounger, soaking up some vitamin D and perhaps a daiquiri. She was as pale as the beach, with almost-white hair and eyebrows. Her mascaraed eyelashes stood out like strands of brown seaweed against the sand.

'Yes, well, it's for my daughter, actually,' Julia answered. 'She'll be coming from Hong Kong. I wanted to know how much it would cost, return?'

'When would she be travelling?'

'We're not sure yet,' Julia said, as if they had been in conversation, she and Jess, and were working it out, rather than Julia herself indulging in a bit of optimistic thinking and jumping the gun. 'Perhaps July or August? But a ballpark figure would do.'

'Certainly, let me have a look.' The girl looked down at her screen, her fingers rapping the keys at an improbable rate. Julia picked up a brochure, and did a bit of travel window shopping while she waited. Which destination would she go to, she thought, if money and time were no object?

The sounds of the rest of the shop – the staff on the phone or moving around, the occasional customer coming in – faded to a background mumble while Julia tried to decide between Bali and Thailand, Mexico and Peru. She had begun to lean heavily towards Peru, when a voice emerged from the mumble. It was a familiar voice, but not one she knew well. She turned to see Luke Benjamin at the table on the other side of the office, talking to the pretty travel agent across from him. His voice had an urgent quality.

'Yes, I know it's not an open ticket, but I can't go back on Saturday, I have to extend the ticket for another ten days,' he was saying.

'You see, sir, when you left New Zealand, it was low season. You got the low season rate for both legs, because your return flight was on the last day of low season. Now, you see, Monday is the start of what we call shoulder season. That's the shoulder between low and high. That means the tickets are more expensive.'

'Well, how much more?' Luke said, sounding weary.

'I'd have to check, but at least a hundred pounds, perhaps more.'

'I'm sure my dad will pay the difference.'

'Except he can't, you see, because this ticket that you got was a special offer. You can't change it. You see here, in the fine print, it says "under any circumstances". That means, you know, any circumstances, at all...'

Julia was watching shamelessly by now. Luke had his back to her, his shoulders slumped in an attitude of defeat.

'...except for a death in the family,' the travel agent continued.

Luke raised his head and said, sadly, 'That's exactly it, there *was* a death in the family. That's why I have to stay. My mother, she died. The memorial is on Sunday.'

The travel agent looked at him and said, 'Well, why didn't you say so?'

'I just... I didn't think... You said "any circumstances."'

'Any circumstances except a death in the family. You'd have to have proof, I'm afraid. A death certificate or similar.'

'Okay, I'll ask my dad.'

Luke reached for his phone, and called, looking increasingly desperate as the moments ticked by without an answer. The travel agent eyed him suspiciously.

'He's not there. I will email it. Can you reserve the ticket in the meantime?'

'Ooh, I can't do that. Anyone can come in here and say someone's died.'

Julia could stand it no longer. She got up and walked over. 'I don't mean to interfere, but I happened to overhear. I do know this young man, and as he said, his mother passed away at the weekend, sadly.'

Luke looked up at her in surprise and confusion. He clearly didn't recognise her.

'I met you in the charity shop,' she said.

'Oh. Yes. Thank you,' he muttered, and then to the travel agent, 'You see? She can vouch for me.'

The travel agent looked from Julia to Luke, obviously trying to assess whether this was some sort of elaborate scam, or a genuine case of a dead mother. 'I'm sorry for your loss,' she eventually said, and added something between an explanation and an apology: 'It's my job.'

'Yeah, well...'

'Okay. Under the circumstances, I'll put a temporary extension on the ticket and reserve the new date. Then you can email me a copy of the death certificate when you get home, okay? But if I don't have it by close of business, I'm cancelling it, understood?'

'Yes thanks,' Luke said, including both his travel agent and Julia in his dull gratitude.

Julia gave him a sympathetic smile and went back to the desk where Sandi was waiting with a cost estimate to bring Julia's own child to visit, to repair and strengthen her relationship with her still-living-and-breathing mother, because life was short and precious and unpredictable.

10

Sean was fetching Julia for book club, which had been moved to Fridays at the request of some of the members. Sean and Julia had agreed to leave Leo at her house as a calming and civilising influence on Jake, and walk to the library together. It was by now old news around the village that the doctor and the new resident were an item, so there was no reason not to arrive and leave together, but Julia still felt a bit awkward. She wondered if there was resentment amongst the village ladies of a certain age that the newbie had snagged the good-looking doctor. She was pleased not to have experienced any overt animosity on that score, but was certain there must be some disappointed admirers.

They could rest assured, she hadn't snagged him with her efficient domesticity. It was her turn to bring a savoury snack to the meeting at the library. She had made a spinach and mushroom quiche, which had turned out well, if a little lopsided, but its creation had somehow necessitated the use of every pot, bowl, whisk and spoon she owned. She had just started cleaning up when Jake went mad – madder than usual – indicating the imminent arrival of Leo. Sean was arriving with time to spare to get the dogs settled. Julia had left the door open, and Sean and his dog came in. The kitchen looked as if a bomb had gone off and sprayed cutlery and crockery about the place – now with added excited dogs.

'I'll put them out. Come on, chaps,' Sean said, ushering them out of the kitchen door and into the garden, and closing it behind them. 'Let me give you a hand with the tidy up. We've got plenty of time.'

'Oh, not to worry, it won't take a minute,' Julia said, shoving a handful of cutlery into the dishwasher.

'Half a minute with two,' Sean said, picking up a bowl in each hand and depositing them in the sink. As well as his competence, she appreciated his casual manner. He didn't behave as if he was saving the day, just pitched in calmly without making her feel useless or ashamed.

It wasn't half a minute, but it wasn't too arduous, and it was certainly more pleasant with company, chatting away. Sean had made some progress on a difficult and perplexing case at work that had been worrying him over the past few days – he didn't share names or personal details, of course, but he shared his worry. After sending off bloods and doing some research and chatting with a colleague who was a specialist, he now had a good idea of what might be the cause of his patient's illness. He had a plan for next steps – another test, a new medication.

'It must be very satisfying, working it all out like that,' Julia said. 'Sort of like being a detective. And at the end of it all, you are actually helping someone quite profoundly.'

'It is satisfying. Really, you just follow the protocols, step by step, as you've been trained. But there's often a little spark, something the patient says that niggles you. Or you wake up at night, and realise, maybe this or that is significant.'

'I know the exact feeling; it's wonderful,' she said. 'When there's a problem to be solved, or an issue to be worked out, I sometimes get that flash of insight. Usually just a niggling feeling that something's not right.'

'That you do. It comes from years of experience. In your case, you've been out in the field for a long time – that's why you have such good instincts.'

'Well, mostly... Not always...' Julia wiped the counter around the sink with slow sweeps, thinking about a time her instincts had been wrong, with potentially devastating consequences.

'Are you all right?' Sean asked.

She tossed the damp cloth into the sink, dried her hands on a clean, dry one hanging from the oven door handle, and gave him a smile. 'Yes, fine. We'd better get going.'

She grabbed a jacket off the hook by the door and picked up the plate with the quiche. Sean opened the door and followed her out.

They entered the library on the dot of six – the official start time – and found the rest of the book club already seated, and in full steam of chatter. They broke off to welcome them and admire the quiche. With Sean at her side, Julia held it out proudly, while the others cooed and aahed. It reminded Julia of showing a new baby around the aunties. She and Peter had felt like the first and cleverest parents alive, with the most beautiful baby. The thought made her nostalgic, and a little sad. *Goodness, what has got into you?* she asked herself – as always, employing her dead mother's brisk tone. *You've come over all moody and sentimental the last little while. Time to buck up, Julia. It's a pie, for heaven's sake, not an infant!*

Buck up she did, acknowledging the compliments with a smile and a thank you, and putting the quiche down on the tea table where it joined a plate of lemon bars, the like of which she'd seen many times before.

'Those look good. Your work, Tabitha?'

'Yes, indeed. I try to make something different, but they won't let me!'

'Nooo!' said Pippa. 'We love the lemon bars.'

Sean and Julia took the little two-seater sofa which had clearly been left for them. The elderly library cat, Tabitha Too, occupied the floor space, so that everyone could admire her magnificent stripes without craning their necks.

'Now we're all here, let's get started, shall we?' As the librarian, Tabitha was the official Boss of Book Club, but as Julia teased her, she held the reins of power lightly, and with grace. 'The genre for the month was mysteries, so what have you all read? Who wants to start?'

Dylan, the youngest member in his early twenties, who was slouched in an armchair across from Julia, unfurled his arm and put up his hand. This was unusual. Dylan generally took a while to warm up. He tried to look inconspicuous when there was a call for volunteers, gradually adding a comment here and there until he'd built up enough steam to present a book of his own. He reminded Julia of a documentary she'd seen on sloths. The long limbs and slow movement, the shaggy hair. He even had the slightly close-together round eyes. She was used to it, of course: the lethargy, the shaggy, unkempt look. She'd seen it often enough working in Youth Services. Dylan was a good chap, not troubled or trouble, as far as Julia could see. He was in the library in a book club with a bunch of old folk on a Friday night, for heaven's sake. You didn't get much more wholesome than that.

Tabitha nodded encouragingly towards Dylan and he spoke: 'So I was reading this one, yeah?' He held up a book. 'Really good. This woman was killed on a train, right? There's only ten people on the train. Easy-peasy. But everyone had an alibi. Or so it seemed. But there's a twist, right? Cos not everyone is who you think they are. There's this bloke, right?

The train conductor? And the timing of the train journey didn't work, see? And...'

'Ooooh. Don't say more!' Diane said, making shushing motions with her hands. 'You've sold me. I'll take that, thank you.' Dylan handed it over with a smile and a sort of ducking motion of the head.

The rest of the book club members took turns to talk about the books they'd been reading. Pippa the guide dog puppy foster mum was, to everyone's surprise, a fan of graphic slasher serial killer books. She launched into a harrowing description of the killer's modus operandi in the book she'd been reading, and only stopped when Jane squealed and put her hands over her ears in protest. No one took her recommendation.

Julia herself had fallen into a cosy mystery series, which featured the surprisingly regular and fairly gentle dropping dead of Italian village residents. Sean had read a non-fiction account of a forensics lab in LA, which Julia had already earmarked on his recommendation. The chatter was pleasant and the atmosphere convivial, and then it was time for tea. The club trooped to the tea table and formed something between a crush and a queue, helping themselves to tea and eats, with appropriate voicing of appreciation for the excellence of the latter and the skill of the chefs. Then they filed back to enjoy their spoils from the comfort of the chairs and sofas.

'Speaking of mysteries,' said Jane, in a none-too-subtle segue from literary chatter to gossip, 'did anyone know that poor woman who died at the Spring Fair?'

'Yeah.'

Everyone turned to Dylan, but it seemed he had answered the question to his satisfaction. He went back to his mammoth wedge of quiche, cutting off a big corner and delivering it into his mouth.

'Well, how, Dylan?' Jane asked, a bit tetchily. 'How did you know her?'

He chewed slowly, then swallowed. 'She was the maths teacher at my school.'

'You went to St Martin's?' Pippa asked.

'Yeah. She taught there for ages. Not now, obviously. May she rest in peace.'

'How did you find her?' asked Jane.

Dylan looked befuddled by the question. 'Well, I dunno. She was a teacher. She was okay. A bit grumpy – sort of sarky, like. Strict marker. Took a mark off me once for not doing the line clearly enough between the numerator and denominator in a fraction. A bit of a pain, really, she was. But not so's you'd want to kill her.'

They waited for more, but Dylan had turned his attention to his lemon square. He took a bite and chewed slowly, in a very sloth-like manner. They'd given up any hope of more info, when he added, 'Her son was in my class. Luke. Poor guy. Imagine having your mum teaching in the school. Must be weird. Never saw him speak to her, not once. Flat-out ignored his mum at school for five years. Weird.'

Julia and Sean walked in silence for a few minutes, enjoying the cool evening air and the darkness. Julia loved how rich with sound the country night was – the tiny croaks and squeaks, rustles and sighs of the birds and beasts and trees and air. A car disturbed the gentle soundscape, and she felt quite annoyed at the driver for spoiling things.

Sean spoke: 'We haven't even talked about your day. What did you do, apart from quiche-making?'

'Well, I wrote to Jess. She sent me an email a few days ago, saying she might come to visit. So I wrote to tell her how happy I would be to see her.' Julia paused and threaded her arm through his, linking at the elbows, and added, 'I told her about you.'

Sean made the gruff 'aherm' noise he sometimes made when he was slightly discombobulated. 'Ah, well, that's, er, that's good. I hope she comes. *Aherm*. I'd like to meet her. And I know you miss her.'

'I really do. I even priced the tickets. A bit premature, but I was passing the travel agent and I popped in just to see... They're expensive, but doable, and I'm sure Peter will share the cost.'

'It's good that you and Peter are so reasonable about everything. It makes things easier all round, and for Jess, too. I'm sure she appreciates it.'

'It was hard for her, us splitting up. Even though she was off at uni, and even though Peter and I weren't especially acrimonious. It was a real shock for her and she dealt with it by running away. I'm hoping this visit will happen, and that it will give her a chance to reconnect with both her parents separately. And to meet our significant others.'

'Well, I'm flattered.'

'I meant Jake,' she said, giving him a nudge.

'I meant Leo!'

She gave his arm a squeeze and they laughed and walked on. Julia's mind wandered over the past day and she remembered something she hadn't told him.

'Oh, and I bumped into Luke while I was at the travel agent's. Ursula's son, Dylan's former classmate, as we discovered this evening. Poor chap was trying to change his return ticket to New Zealand for a later date so he can be at the memorial on Sunday, but they were giving him the run-around.'

'That sounds unpleasant for him, dealing with that so soon after his mum's death.'

'Yes. But I think he got it done. I put in a word.'

'I have no doubt,' Sean said. His eyes teased, letting it be known that he knew she had been interfering again. Which of course she had been, but it was for a good cause.

Julia thought of Luke's dad, Robert, and DC Farmer's suspicions. She wondered if the police had found anything to implicate the husband in the murder. She hoped not, for Luke's sake. Robert had been quite protective of Luke, quite tender, when she'd seen them in the shop. She felt sad thinking of the two of them packing up Ursula's things, just days after her death. It would be awful if Robert was the killer.

There was that niggling feeling she and Sean had been talking about on their way to book club. A kind of fizzing itch of the brain, the notion that something was not quite right. She'd been feeling it there, at the back of her head, most of the evening. Since Dylan had said that thing about the timing of journeys not working out, when he was talking about his book.

Because, she thought now, that was what the problem was with Luke's story. It was the timing. It seemed to her that everything had happened too quickly – the death, Luke's arrival, the clothes.

'Sean, there's something off about Luke's story. Hear me out, tell me if I'm going crazy.'

'Okay. Often talking things out helps,' said Sean with a smile.

'So when Walter told me about Luke, the son, he said: "He flew home as soon as his dad told him about his mum's death." But Ursula died on Sunday. If it's true Luke left as soon as he heard, the absolute earliest he could have booked would have been Sunday night, right? Even that would be a heck of a stretch. Say he booked right away and managed to leave on Monday. It's twenty-four to forty-eight hours to get here. He would have arrived Tuesday at the very earliest. Luke and Robert had packed up Ursula's things to get them delivered to Second Chances on Wednesday morning first thing.'

Sean nodded along at her timeline, doing the maths, a little frown on his forehead.

'Doesn't this seem strange to you?' Julia asked.

'More than strange, it seems impossible,' Sean said, after a pause. 'I reckon he could just about have managed it if every single flight lined up, but realistically, not doable.'

'Let's say everything lined up, there's another thing that doesn't make sense. Surely he wouldn't have booked to fly back three or four days later? He's not nipping over from Calais for the weekend. It's New Zealand, for heaven's sake. The longest of long hauls. And when he booked he would have known there would be things to sort out, and a memorial, of course. Even if he had work to consider, he would have booked for a week at least, more like two.'

'You're right on all counts. It doesn't add up. The most obvious explanation is that Walter Farmer got it wrong. Misheard, or misunderstood.'

'No,' said Julia, after thinking for a moment. 'Robert said the same, I remember. When they came into Second Chances, he said that his son had just come from New Zealand. And then he told Walter that he had come as soon as he heard about Ursula. And if he had come just for the memorial, well then, he wouldn't be having to extend the ticket, would he? He would have booked it for long enough, and wouldn't be having to prove to the travel agent that his mother had died. I'm pretty sure Robert is lying. Luke came before Ursula died.'

'Why would he lie, though?'

'That's the thing, isn't it?' said Julia. 'The only possible reason Robert has to lie is that he doesn't want the police to know that Luke was in England when Ursula died. He's lying to protect Luke.'

Sean and Julia looked at each other, absorbing the implications of this.

'Well, in that case,' said Sean, 'I think you need to talk to Hayley Gibson.'

11

Going to talk to Hayley Gibson was the correct thing to do, she was sure of it. Well, almost sure. But...

Julia took a sip of her Earl Grey tea, replaced the cup in the saucer and the saucer on the kitchen table, and considered her reluctance to approach the detective inspector.

It was entirely circumstantial and unintended that Julia had found herself enmeshed in a number of police investigations. After the most recent case, in which best-selling author Vincent Andrews had been killed and Julia had helped solve the crime, Hayley had made it clear that – grateful as she was to have the killer behind bars – she didn't encourage civilian interference in police matters: 'I appreciate your help. You've got good instincts about people and their motives. But when you nose about, you run the risk of compromising police investigations.'

Julia knew Hayley was right. She had spent decades working in the system, trying to sort out problems, fix what was broken. She was something of a professional interferer. It was a hard habit to break. But she had retired from social work with that very intention – to break the habit. She had her work cut out for her, raising chickens and walking dogs and baking fairly respectable scones and enjoying the company of her attractive late-life boyfriend. She had no desire to poke her nose into police business. Except that now here she was again.

Julia took a bite of her toast and marmalade, followed by another sip of her tea, and thought about her situation. She hadn't interfered this time. Not really. She'd just overheard a few things and put them together. She wouldn't speak to Robert or Luke. She would go to Hayley with her suspicions about their dodgy timeline, and let her handle it.

No time like the present, she thought, fetching her phone from its place on the sideboard. She'd get that off her plate and go about her Saturday. Hayley's phone rang and rang and went to voicemail. In her most official Detective Inspector voice, she instructed callers to not leave a voice message, but rather send an SMS. Julia typed a quick note:

Had a thought re: Ursula investigation. You might want to check when Luke Benjamin left NZ and arrived in UK. Timeline seems a bit off. Give me a call if you like.

She felt a little better after that. She called Jake, and offered him the opportunity to accompany her into the village. There was a farmers' market on the green outside the church on the third Saturday of the month – which this happened to be. She would pick up on fruit and vegetables for the week. 'Not really your preferred menu option, but we might be able to get you a bit of sausage or some such if you're on your best behaviour,' she said.

Jake seemed agreeable to that notion. One thing you could say for Labradors – they were agreeable by nature and generally up for any outing you proposed. All the more so if the outing involved sausage.

It certainly was a lovely day for a walk: warm and bright and fragrant with the scent of jasmine and the promise of spring. Jake and Julia set off at a brisk pace. With her basket over one arm and her dog's lead in the other, Julia felt happy and purposeful and at home in the village community.

The roads and paths were familiar to her now, and her feet took her almost unconsciously where she needed to be. She passed the houses, noting new developments as she went – Betty Pringle's roses were looking magnificent. Someone should trim that hedge on the corner of the close; it was sticking into the pavement and might scratch a passer-by. And was that a new bike outside number forty-four? She passed the dry cleaner's and the off-licence and the police station. Once again, she commended herself on her no-interference policy.

Jake tugged at his lead, pulling in the direction of a tall man sitting on a bench at the edge of a park just up from the police station, stooped over, his elbows on his knees, his head in his hands. He appeared to be in some kind of distress. Despite being a galumphing fool much of the time, Jake was surprisingly sensitive to people's distress, and would often bound over to a crying child to comfort them with his chocolatey good-heartedness. Jake now slipped from Julia's grasp to run over to the fellow and push his velvet nose onto his lap.

The man straightened in alarm at the intrusion, and then reached down and stroked Jake's soft, glossy head and ears. A small smile broke over his stricken face. Julia recognised the pale, narrow face, the steel-grey hair. It was Robert Benjamin.

'Hello, good boy,' Robert said, giving Jake a pat. He looked around for an owner and saw Julia. 'Oh, hello?' His voice was tentative, as if he knew he'd seen her before, but couldn't place her.

'Hello. Sorry about the dog, he's very friendly. I'm Julia Bird. We met at the charity shop. I work there.'

'Oh yes, of course. You helped me with the clothes, I'm sorry.'

He shifted slightly on the bench to give her space to sit

down. Jake had calmed down and was sitting at Robert's feet, leaning against his leg. Robert was still stroking the dog's silky ear absent-mindedly.

'Don't apologise,' Julia said, sitting down. 'How are you holding up?'

'Well you know... Doing what we can. It's not easy. And the memorial's tomorrow.'

'I heard. Did Luke manage to change his flight?'

He turned to face her in surprise. 'How did you...? Oh right, were you the lady who vouched for him at the travel agent? He mentioned that. Yes, they made a provisional booking and I sent the death certificate. He's got another week or so with me. Thank you.'

'It was nothing. Poor guy, it's not easy having to deal with all the practicalities as well as processing the loss and grief.'

Robert looked at her gratefully. 'That's it exactly. You can't believe the paperwork, the organisation. And of course the police inquiry is stressful.'

Stressful because they've lied to the police, thought Julia, or stressful in the usual way these things are?

'Well, I'm glad Luke will be able to stay a little longer so you have each other for support through all of that, and in your grief,' she said aloud.

'It's been very hard for him.'

'Devastating to lose a parent, and in such awful circumstances. But it's good that he was able to be here for the memorial. Brings closure.'

'Closure. Yes.' Robert looked uncomfortable with the idea of closure.

'It always seems so sad, doesn't it, for someone who has been away to come home only after a loved one's death?' said Julia, putting her question that was designed to entrap in as gentle a way as possible.

Robert gave no comment.

'Isn't that what happened? I thought that was what you told the police, that he flew back as soon as he heard.'

'Yes,' said Robert, but he didn't look up at Julia as he spoke. Instead, he seemed focused on Jake's soft ears. 'That's what I said.'

'Only that couldn't be right, could it? All the way from New Zealand in – what, a day?' said Julia, keeping her voice gentle and even. 'Luke came back before Ursula even stepped foot in that maze, didn't he, Robert?'

Julia hoped that Robert couldn't tell how her heart was beating beneath her calm exterior. She felt in her bag for her phone, wondering if she could call Hayley while she spoke, before Robert ran away – or worse! The police station was just here, if things went pear-shaped, she told herself.

'I don't know what you mean,' said Robert, his whole body still.

'The flight times, Robert. And the special flight offer. Luke was already in England when Ursula died. And I have to be honest, I can only see one reason that you'd be lying about it.'

Robert sighed deeply.

'You're right. It was a stupid lie,' he said. 'But you know how it is, I'm sure, when it comes to protecting your family.'

'So you lied to protect Luke?' Julia said, once again working hard on that calm, even voice. The man was about to spill the beans – to admit that his son had murdered his own mother! She hoped that his confession wouldn't be invalid hearsay because it was happening on a park bench, rather than in the police station. This was exactly why Hayley didn't like her interfering!

'To protect Luke, yes, in a way,' said Robert slowly, as if he was thinking about it. 'But more to protect Ursula. So nobody would know.'

'Protect her? So nobody would know that her own son killed her?' said Julia, hardly able to mask her surprise.

'Killed her?' said Robert, equally surprised, and finally turning to look at Julia. 'What are you talking about? Luke would never kill anyone. And besides, he was with me in London when Ursula died. We were watching the big rugby game live at Twickenham.'

'Were you? You and Luke?'

'Yes!' he said, reaching into his jacket pocket. 'Here, look. I still have the tickets on my phone.' He flicked quickly through the screens with an air of desperation, and then held the phone up with an air of triumph. 'See? Twickenham, 2 p.m. England vs the Wallabies. Look, got great tickets for a father and son treat. Right on the halfway line. You don't get better than that.'

Julia glanced at the tickets, which seemed to bear out his story. The date and time were correct, at least. Although just because he had the tickets on his phone, it didn't mean that he and Luke had actually gone to the game. Before she could think this through properly and formulate a question, Robert was back on the defensive.

'Luke would never kill anybody! Certainly not Ursula, even if they didn't... You've got completely the wrong idea. What would make you think such a thing?'

'Because you lied about when he arrived in England. And then right now, you said that you were protecting him.'

'I was!' said Robert, his soft voice getting quite loud. 'I was. But not because he killed her, but because I didn't want anyone to know how bad it really was between Luke and Ursula!' This last was almost shouted, and Julia was sure that whatever it was would be all around the village by tea time.

'What?' she asked, confused. 'What do you mean? Bad in what way?'

Robert sighed and shook his head sadly. 'They didn't get on at all. In fact, they were estranged the last few years.'

Julia could hear the pain in Robert's voice, and almost automatically slipped back into the empathetic listening habits of her earlier career. 'Those teenage and early adult years can be difficult for parents and children, can't they? The children wanting their freedom and agency, the parents holding on to their power. It's not an easy time.'

Robert shook his head slowly. 'No, it's not. And Ursula, for all her good qualities, was not an easy woman. She had firm positions, and didn't deal well with opposition. She was always in the right. She liked to win. She held grudges. And when it came to Luke...' Robert paused, staring at Jake, who was staring back at him, thoroughly enjoying the extended ear scratch he was getting from the distraught man.

Julia kept her eyes ahead of her and waited, giving Robert the space to talk.

'When it came to Luke, she just wouldn't give any quarter. From when he was little, she was very controlling. She wanted the best for him, I suppose, to keep him on the straight and narrow, bring him up right as she saw it. But she was harsh and it drove him away. And something happened between Ursula and I – a private marital problem – but Luke caught wind and never forgave her, even though I did. So off he went, all the way to New Zealand, as soon as he was old enough to make that choice. I've always held out hope that they would come back to each other eventually. I thought she would mellow; she'd realise she couldn't control him. And I thought he would be more forgiving as he matured. But now they won't have that chance.'

'How sad for them both that they couldn't reconnect. I'm sure it hurt her, too.' Julia still couldn't work out how this all led to a lie about Luke's whereabouts. 'Did he manage to spend any time with her on this visit? Before she died?'

'No. No, he wasn't ready for that. That's the whole thing. When I bought him a ticket to come and see me, he said he'd come, but he made me promise not to tell her he was here. That was why I'd been in London for the week. There was a trumped-up work visit to explain my absence, plus the rugby game, which I'd said I was going to with mates. But really I was seeing Luke. I'd hoped he would change his mind and agree to a visit to his old home and to see his mum, but he was adamant. He wasn't ready.'

'Poor Luke. It makes her death harder, in some ways, things being so unresolved when she died.'

'Exactly,' Robert said, clearly grateful for her understanding. 'It's devastating. He's angry and confused and sad.'

'The thing is...' Julia trod carefully, keeping her voice neutral. 'The thing is, it will come out, that's for sure, in the course of the investigation. The air ticket, the London trip... If I found out without even trying, the police will find out that Luke arrived here before she died, and not after. They will wonder why he lied about it; why you did. It doesn't look good for Luke, to be honest. If you are telling the truth and Luke did nothing wrong, you have done him no favours with this silly lie.'

'I am telling the truth! He didn't kill her. I was so stupid! I don't know why I lied about his arrival; it just happened. It was an instinct, to protect Ursula from the village gossip, out of respect for her memory. And to protect Luke. I didn't want people to know that they were estranged, that he had come to England and not even seen his mum. It's an awful irony, isn't it – he did come home, he was here when she died. And she never knew it.'

It had seemed impossible that he could look more drawn and pale than he already did, but now the last remaining colour drained from his face.

'How stupid of me. I was trying to protect him, and now I've put him under suspicion. What am I going to do?'

'You need to speak to DI Hayley Gibson. Just tell her what you did, and why. You have to come clean. She's a reasonable person; she'll listen to what you have to say. And Robert, I'm afraid if you don't do it, I'm going to have to do it myself.'

A car pulled up beside them. It was Hayley, as if summoned

by the mention of her name. She got out and stood in front of the two of them, her arms folded across her chest, a cold look on her face.

'I got your message,' she said to Julia, her bright blue eyes boring into her, saying more than the short sentence she had uttered. And, turning to Robert, 'I was on my way to the station. DC Farmer is bringing Luke in.'

'Luke? No! I can explain...'

Hayley opened the car door with a determined flourish: 'You can and you will. Now get in the car.'

12

'I have some questions about rugby,' Julia said, causing Sean to burst out laughing in that hearty Father Christmas laugh he had – *ho, ho, ho*. He put down the spatula he'd been using to shuffle bacon around, turned off the pan, and came to sit down next to her at the kitchen table.

'Oh, have you now? Well, there's a thing. Allow me to be of service. Just don't ask me why the ball is that shape. No one knows.'

'That wasn't my question, although it's a patently ridiculous shape for a ball. I have no idea what they were thinking.'

'Well, if that wasn't your question, the answer is yes, it's true they can only pass the ball backwards. It does seem like an inefficient way to get the ball to the other side of the pitch, I grant you, but the ways of men are mysterious, and occasionally idiotic.'

'It wasn't that either,' she said, laughing with him, somewhat against her will. 'It's a question about the lines.'

'Ah, so, it's three points for a try, and then if there's conversion, which is to say...'

'Sean! Seriously. It's about a murder.'

The toaster popped, but they both ignored it. Their lunch of BLTs could wait.

'That would be the murder you swore off interfering in, would it?' Sean said, putting his arm around her shoulders and hugging her to him. She loved his easy, affectionate manner, and the way he could tease her without mocking so she could never take offence.

'The very one,' she said, swatting his chest with the back of her hand. 'Except I'm not interfering, merely checking an alibi. Robert said he and Luke were at a particular game at Twickenham. If he's telling the truth, they couldn't have been in Berrywick killing Ursula.'

'They're suspects?'

'I didn't think so, but Hayley's taken Luke in for questioning. And Robert has been less than truthful about their whereabouts, which doesn't make things look good for them. As it turns out, there was a lot of bad blood between Luke and Ursula. Serious estrangement, resentment, pain. The kind of thing that could lead to violence. I know that.'

'But you don't think either of them did it?'

'My instincts are that neither of them has it in them. It's a long way from family friction to strangulation, and Robert seemed genuinely astonished at the notion of Luke being physically violent. Maybe I'm naive, but I'd like to believe they were at the rugby, like he said.'

Sean nodded. 'Well, I do believe your instincts are more often than not reliable. But you need more than instincts, here. How do you plan to prove or disprove that they were at the rugby? You said you had a rugby-related question?'

'Yes. I saw the tickets on Robert's phone. It was a match against the Wallabies at Twickenham on Saturday, just as he said.'

'Ah yes, we missed it because of the Spring Fair. I watched it when I got home, remember? A fair running game, although there were one or two fumbles that might have cost us dearly, you see, when...'

Julia raised her eyebrows and held her palms up in front of her face to convey the message that she didn't want a full analysis of the play.

'Right,' Sean said.

'Anyway, the date and time are correct,' she continued. 'But anyone can buy a ticket, can't they? It doesn't mean they went to the game.'

'Could have given it to me, in that case. Bloody waste,' Sean muttered. 'Expensive, those tickets are.'

Julia ignored him and continued, 'Robert could have bought the tickets to create an alibi. It might have been a set-up to protect himself and Luke in case of an investigation. He said they were sitting at the halfway line. So I thought I might be able to find out somehow if they were there, or if their seats were empty. I don't know, phone the stadium, or maybe the television station, see if I could get a recording. Something like that.'

'No need for that, necessarily,' Sean said cheerfully. 'Grab your computer.'

'How...?'

'Go and get it. If they were at the halfway line, there's a chance the camera would have picked them up when the teams came out of the tunnel. And even if they aren't on camera then, there was a controversial scrum on the halfway line, so they might show up on the highlights reel. I still think that the ref was wrong, myself, but they replayed it all several times from several angles, so there's a good chance we'll see your guys if they were there.'

Julia grabbed her laptop from the dresser and opened it, impatiently entering her password which was – to her shame and no doubt to the great detriment of her online security – *Jakey1!*.

'If you pass it over, I'll see if I can find the highlights from that match.'

She turned the computer towards Sean, and he tapped away for a few minutes, before turning it back to centre, so they could both watch. 'Here you go. Highlights.'

Julia pressed play and watched intently, her cursor hovering over the pause button.

'Okay, here we go,' Sean said, as the two teams prepared to go into a scrum. 'See there, how that guy at the back seems to collapse on purpose? And now, wait, look at that... The other team's hooker definitely meant to punch him! It wasn't a mistake! I knew it!'

But Julia had no interest in the pile of men on the field. She was watching the stands.

The crowd were on their feet, yelling at the field. Really, thought Julia, people did get very worked up about sports. The camera panned the crowd, taking in the looks of rage and confusion.

'There!' She hit pause, catching Robert open-mouthed in full cry, his eyes closed. Next to him, Luke, half-turned at an awkward angle, his right arm raised in a fist. 'That's them.'

'Excellent work, Mrs Bird!' Sean said, with real admiration. 'You've proved your point and their innocence. Now, shall we have our lunch?'

'Not yet,' Julia said, in a panicked tone, reaching for her phone. 'I need to get hold of Hayley, and get Robert and Luke out of that police station.' She was already scrolling her contacts as she said it. Hitting dial, she put the phone to her ear.

'Voicemail!' she said. 'I'll try the station.'

'You do that, and I'll see to lunch,' said Sean, but Julia was hardly listening to him.

More scrolling. The phone to her ear again.

'Walter! Hi, Julia Bird here. Fine, fine, thanks. Is Hayley there...? With whom...? Come on, Walter, I was there when she took Robert in, so it's not as if it's a big secret... I understand. No, I'm not expecting you to give out information, it's just... Absolutely, I understand.

'Well, could I tell you, and you tell her? Urgently...? Right, thank you. Luke and Robert were in London at the rugby match when Ursula was killed. I've seen a video of the match, and they're visible in the stands. I'm sending the video link now. It means neither Luke nor Robert could have killed Ursula. Hayley needs to release them today, as soon as possible. It's Ursula's memorial tomorrow, they need to get home...'

The tension in her body relaxed and she said, 'Thanks, Walter, I appreciate that. Goodbye.'

She ended the call and pulled the computer towards her, copying the link to the video and sending it to both Hayley and Walter. She closed the laptop and pushed it away from her with a sigh of relief.

'All sorted?' Sean asked, setting her plate down in front of her.

'Yes, thank goodness. He's going to get Hayley right now, they'll take a look at the clip, and get Robert and Luke released asap.'

The smell of the fried bacon suddenly hit her, rendering her ravenous. She looked down at the sandwich: the perfectly toasted wholemeal, generously buttered and topped with the crispy rashers, thinly sliced tomato and her own garden lettuce peeking out of the side, under a generous grinding of black pepper. Sean had cut the sandwich perfectly on the diagonal. A table napkin had been placed next to the plate.

'Thank you,' she said, looking up at him with gratitude. He looked down at her, and she knew that he knew her thanks was not just for the sandwich, but for everything.

'My pleasure,' he said, looking rather pleased with himself. He put an identical sandwich in the place across from her and fetched two glasses of cold water that he'd poured from a jug in the fridge and left on the counter. He placed one in front of each of them, and sat down.

She took a bite of the BLT. It was the perfect combination of salty and fresh, buttery and bready.

'This is wonderful,' she said. 'Just wonderful.'

They ate in silence, chewing contemplatively, each in their own thoughts. A clucking, squawking sound filtered in through the window, and into Julia's head. It was a sound she recognised as that of a triumphant hen who had just laid an egg, and it had clearly shaken Sean from his reveries too, because he spoke: 'This might sound a bit strange, but...' He paused, and Julia looked at him expectantly. 'But I was thinking that I would like to go to Ursula Benjamin's memorial on Sunday. I didn't know her, but we did find her, after all. I examined her, felt for her pulse. I feel sort of connected. As if I should pay my respects. Is that peculiar?'

'No, not at all. In fact it makes perfect sense. You want to sort of close things off with her.'

'That's it exactly.'

'I think you should go, if that's how you feel.'

'I don't suppose... Well...?'

Julia sighed on the inside, reluctantly giving up her fantasy of downloading the fifth novel in her Italian murder mystery series and retiring to the sofa for the rest of the weekend. On the outside, she said evenly, 'Would you like me to come with you to the memorial?'

Sean beamed his crinkly Sean Connery smile, and nodded. 'Yes, Julia. Yes, I would.'

13

Sean and Julia drove together to St Martin's in Edgely, where Ursula's memorial was to be held in the school hall.

Sean drove, and from the co-pilot seat, Julia pointed out spring highlights. 'Lambs!' she said when they passed a field of sheep with their tiny doubles moored alongside them. 'Aren't they darling?' Then: 'Strawberries!' as they passed a pick-your-own strawberry farm. 'Let's come here when they're in season and pick some.' Later: 'Hawk,' pointing at a large bird brooding on a phone wire. 'Or a falcon. Some sort of bird of prey, anyway, I never know the difference.'

'Giant teacup,' Sean offered, as they passed a garden centre with a cut-out of a huge orange cup and saucer advertising its tea room. 'We should stop there on the way back. I've been meaning to get to the nursery all week. I need to get my summer vegetables in. I think we're done with the cold, don't you?'

Fifteen minutes later they were parked outside the school – a stone building, its golden stone façades forming three triangular peaks, each topped with a small and ancient-looking stone cross. It looked absolutely nothing like the big modern comprehensives that Julia had been accustomed to in her work in London.

A car had drawn up ahead of them, and another stopped right behind them. From the sombre clothing, Julia assumed the occupants were going to the memorial too. She herself was wearing a smartish dress for the first time in she didn't know how long, and a pair of rather good pumps, to which her feet were shockingly unaccustomed. She hoped there wouldn't be too much standing about.

Sean and Julia got out of the car, nodded to their fellow memorial-goers, and followed them through the gates and along a path that took them through a paved quad with classrooms along the sides, to a large stone hall at the end.

'We're a bit early,' said Sean. 'Should we wait outside? Nicer in the garden than in the school hall.'

It was. Bees were going bonkers in a bank of purple rhododendrons that were so large and lush, they would not have been out of place in some primal rainforest. Doubtless, a battalion of gardeners served them lashings of compost and fertiliser to ensure their good health. Julia and Sean stopped at a bench next to a camellia bush, similarly laden with flowers, these ones dense and white. A trickle of people passed through in twos and threes. A group of students walked past, wearing their grey school uniforms and blazers. All appeared to be heading to the memorial.

A familiar figure loped in and caught Julia's eye. It was Dylan from book club. She gave him a little wave and he came over.

'Hey, Julia, Dr Sean.'

'Hi, Dylan. We could have given you a lift, but I didn't know you were coming.'

'Yeah, well. I wasn't sure, but then I thought, like, you know… I mean, Mrs Benjamin wasn't my fave. But I guess Luke might want some familiar faces around. My mum dropped me off.'

'That's good of you. I'm sure Luke will appreciate it.'

'Oh, there he is. I'm gonna go... Catch you later.' And Dylan wandered off to the door of the chapel, where Luke was standing pale-faced and awkward in an ill-fitting blazer that might have been his dad's.

Inside, it was a small crowd that had gathered for Ursula's memorial. Julia caught sight of Candy, the nice young woman from the cake stall at the fair. As memorials went, Ursula Benjamin's was not typical. One might have expected her only son to say a few words, as well as perhaps some colleagues and friends, even some of her maths pupils. Instead, only two people spoke. As Robert approached the podium, Julia saw that his hands were shaking, the typed cards with his speech on trembling slightly. Poor man – what a lot he had gone through in the last few days. Julia was pleased that Hayley had been able to look at the rugby footage and rule him and Luke out as suspects. At least that was one less burden.

Robert started by speaking about Ursula's early life – where she was born, her life at home with her parents and siblings, her university years. He talked of their wedding, their happiness at Luke's arrival, and then his pride in their son. Julia wasn't sure if it was just because she knew the full story, but it felt to her that what he wasn't saying – a wonderful mother, will be greatly missed, the usual platitudes – spoke louder than what he was saying.

Finally, Robert put aside the cue cards, and said, 'Ursula wasn't an easy woman. She had strong opinions, and that often upset people. She didn't make friends easily. The truth of it is that many of you here today didn't really know her, but are here from a sense of duty. But she didn't deserve to die so young and so violently. I've lost my wife, my companion of twenty-five years. Maybe not all of you would have chosen her, but I did. And now she's gone.'

It was awfully touching in its honesty, and Julia found herself wiping away a tear with the clean handkerchief that Sean quietly handed her.

The head of the school, one David Schofield, spoke after Robert. He spoke with pride of the success of the school's maths programme under Mrs Benjamin – she had had students in the top maths rankings in the country every year, he said, for over a decade. Other than that, his tribute seemed surprisingly impersonal and dry. Having waxed fulsomely about Ursula's excellent results, he told the gathering about her excellent attendance record – she had never missed a day, apparently, in her decades-long service as a maths teacher at the school. He did not mention her impending retirement, or any extension thereof. He mentioned that grief was a hard burden for a family, and that he himself had lost his beloved wife just six months previously, and then ended by simply saying, 'Our sympathies go out to Robert and Luke on their loss.' And then, 'The school choir will lead us in a hymn.'

The piano started up and the small group of uniformed teens that had passed them on the way in started to sing:

The Lord's my Shepherd
I'll not want...

Where the memorial had been rather bare and stilted, the clear, young voices were very moving. The rest of the gathering joined in, struggling to stay in tune, the pitch too high or too low for their voices, as always seemed the case in Julia's experience of group singing.

Yea, though I walk in death's dark vale,
Yet will I fear no ill...

Julia thought of Ursula's last moments. She would have felt fear, all right, of that there was no doubt, as the rope – or had it been hands? – had closed around her neck. Had she tried to call for help, in death's dark vale? Had she been thinking of her estranged son in those moments, wishing for connection?

The song ended and Robert stood up again and invited everyone to join them for a sandwich and cup of tea in the school quad. And that was that; the memorial was over.

Julia found herself standing with Sean and Dylan in the quad, eating a small triangular sandwich consisting of an ungenerous grating of processed orange cheese and a slice of tasteless tomato on thin white bread.

'That was my first memorial service, other than my granny's funeral,' said Dylan. 'Is that how they usually are? I'd imagined people weeping and wailing and rending their clothes, like.'

Julia smiled – Dylan always enjoyed the more dramatic and gothic choices at book club.

'It was a rather different one,' she said, trying to be diplomatic. 'I suppose it's hard to know what to say when someone dies. And by the sounds of things Ursula was... Complicated. One gets the feeling she wasn't easy to get to know, or easy to be with. Terribly sad, really.'

'Well, she was an odd fish,' said Dylan, nodding in his slow way. 'I can't say that I'll miss her. But as Luke's dad said, nobody should die like that. Even if they're, you know...' His voice tailed off.

'Even if they're what?' said Julia. 'How was she when she taught you? You said she was strange, but how?'

'I dunno. I've been thinking about her these last few days. What with her dead, you know? And now that I'm a grown-up, I can see things a bit different. She was good at explaining things. A good teacher. That said, the way she treated me wasn't right, I see now.'

'The way she treated you?' Sean asked, his eyebrows furrowed.

'Yeah. She was, I dunno... Maybe a bully? She started really picking on me at the beginning of the year that she taught me. I was a small lad, a bit of a late bloomer, y'know. She'd make comments about that. And call me stupid if I got something wrong. But I might've been small, but I was nobody's fool. Luckily I was a cocky lad, spoke back when she had a go. And my folks had my back. She soon left me alone. Moved on.' This was the longest speech they'd heard from Dylan, but it wasn't finished. After a pause, he added, 'I've noticed that bullies need a certain type of victim.'

'That's a very insightful observation, Dylan,' said Julia. 'It's exactly what I've noticed in my work.'

'Yeah,' said Dylan. 'But tell that to poor Marcus Featherstone, the lad she started bullying after me. He was a different sort of chap altogether. Gentle guy, sweet-natured and kind of nervy. He left the school, you know. They could say what they liked, but I always thought it was Mrs Benjamin what drove him to leave. It was a real waste – he was a clever chap. I thought he'd go off to uni, and now he's working in that Edgely Garden Centre. You know, the one with the big teacup outside?'

Dylan popped the last corner of an egg sandwich into his mouth and then drained the remains of his tea. 'Better go chat to my mate,' he said, looking over to where Luke was standing across the lawn. 'It's what I'm here for after all. Cheers, Julia, Dr Sean. See you at book club.'

And with that he sloped off in his languid way, leaving the older couple with quite a lot to think about.

14

The long rows of seedling trays provoked in Julia a cheering sense of possibility. It made her happy to think that all these little green clusters of leaves would one day be heads of lettuce, fragrant basil plants, and healthy tomato bushes laden with fruit. All they needed was the right spot with enough sun, enough rain, a bit of loving care, and they would thrive and grow into their full potential. Like children, she thought. Children needed light and love from the adults in their lives. She hated to think of children being badly treated by adults in authority, as many of her clients had been, and as Dylan and his friend had been by Ursula, if the story today was to be believed.

Sean had taken a trolley and wandered off, determinedly filling it up with pots of shrubs and trays of seedlings and bags of fertiliser and compost. They'd agreed that Julia would have a look around and they'd meet up at the car when they'd finished. They might pop into the tea room for a bite to eat. The sandwiches at the memorial had been less than satisfying.

Julia was determined to vigilantly avoid any nursery shopping accidents – one could so easily slip off the rails and give in to every pretty thing, to the detriment of the bank balance – but she picked up a tray of mixed lettuces, telling herself they were not a random impulse purchase, but a necessary addition to the vegetable garden that would be very handy for quick pickings of salad greens.

'Can I get a trolley for you, ma'am?' asked a slight young man whose hair matched his orange garden centre shirt to an uncanny degree. 'Do you need any fertiliser or compost for your seedlings?'

'Oh thank you, no need for a trolley. This is all I'm taking for today. But thank you...' She looked at his large metal name tag, which had *Marcus* printed in big green letters next to a shiny green leaf. 'You're Marcus?' she asked, with a nod to his name tag.

'Yes, ma'am,' he said, tapping the tag with his fingernail, giving off a metallic *ting*. 'Marcus Featherstone, at your service.'

'That's such a strange coincidence. I was just this afternoon with Dylan Baker. I told him I was coming to the Garden Centre and he mentioned that his friend Marcus worked here. And here you are.'

'Here I am,' he said with an easy smile. 'Small world, innit?'

'Yes indeed. This part of it, anyway. I saw Luke Benjamin too – I suppose you would know him as well?'

'Oh yes, we were all at school together. Long time ago now.' The smile faded a little as Marcus said it.

'It was the memorial for Luke's mother, Ursula Benjamin.'

'I heard she died. Murdered. I'm sorry for Luke's loss. It's never easy to lose a parent, no matter how.'

'Yes, awful business. She taught you, did she? Mrs Benjamin?'

'Yes, for a bit. I left the school in Year Ten. That was a few years ago.' Marcus turned as if to go, and then turned back: 'Funny thing, I haven't spoken about St Martin's and Mrs Benjamin in, I dunno, a year or two, and then just a few weeks back, someone came asking about her, and then I read about her death in the paper, of course, and now here you are.'

'That is a strange coincidence.' Who on earth could have been asking about Ursula, Julia wondered, and how could she find out.

'How's Dylan?' Marcus asked, changing the subject.

'He is very well. He's a good chap, Dylan. He went along to the memorial as a friendly face for Luke, which I thought was kind of him, seeing as Luke hadn't had the best experience with his late mother.'

'No, neither did I. She was a good teacher, but not an easy person. In fact, it was because of her that I...' Marcus began, and then seemed to stop himself saying more.

'Left the school?'

'I don't want to speak ill of the dead, and it's all water under the bridge now,' he said, taking the tray of seedlings from her. 'Shall we take these to the till?'

Julia nodded and they walked alongside one another, winding their way between the tables of seedlings. 'That's very decent of you.'

'Just doing my job.'

'I meant the not speaking ill of the dead part. From what I hear, Ursula could be quite nasty if she took against someone, and that's really not acceptable in a teacher.'

'Are you a teacher yourself?' he asked.

'Social worker,' she said. 'Youth Services. I'm retired though. Just last year.'

'Yeah well, you're right about adults picking on kids, it's not acceptable. And Mrs Benjamin was a mean woman who was really horrible to me, and other kids. I wasn't the top of the class, and I was also the smallest boy.'

He was indeed still diminutive. Hardly taller than Julia, and fine boned, with small hands and feet.

'She had a go at me about all of it. And like I told the other guy, the school didn't do anything about it, even when I went to the headteacher. First I thought he was going to help me, but then he did nothing. It was wrong. But I've done the work on that. Thanks to a social worker, in fact. Where I'm at now, I think Mrs Benjamin almost did me a favour.'

'Really?'

'I left the school in the end. It was hard. I had planned on engineering, but I struggled a bit once I left St Martin's. Poor self-esteem, got involved with the usual troublesome teenage stuff, smoked a bit of weed, messed about with the bad lads. I got into trouble and met this great social worker – reminds me a bit of you, actually. Nosy, but in an okay way. And he was a bloke. Anyway, I pulled myself together, went to a good college, a totally different kind of school that suited me better. And now I'm studying horticulture at uni and working here part-time, and I'm engaged to a lovely woman. Milly, she's a yoga teacher. Local girl, she lives over in Hayfield, got her own little yoga studio there and everything. We're going to get married when I graduate. It's all worked out.'

They were at the till now, and Marcus handed over Julia's seedlings to his colleague, whose name tag read *MAGGY*. He waited while Julia paid, and carried the tray to the car, even though Julia insisted it wasn't necessary.

'There you go, ma'am. Full sun, now, and they should be ready for the first picking in a few weeks.'

'Thanks for your help, Marcus. It was a pleasure to meet you. You're a very impressive fellow. Good luck with your studies.'

'Good to meet you too, Mrs...?'

'Bird.'

'Mrs Bird.'

As he turned to go, Julia called after him. 'Marcus,' she said. 'The other guy, the one who asked about Ursula Benjamin, who was he?'

'A reporter. Said he was writing a story about St Martin's. Bullying, kids leaving. Someone had told him I'd left the school suddenly and he wanted to talk to me about what happened. He asked questions about Mr Schofield.'

'What did you say?'

'Same thing I told you. That Mrs Benjamin wasn't a nice lady, that I complained but the head didn't seem to care. I left the school. I've moved on. It wasn't a long conversation cos I was at work.'

Sean was trundling towards them with an overflowing trolley. The man definitely had a shopping problem when it came to plants. He gave Julia a cheery wave, which she returned.

'Marcus, do you remember what paper this reporter was from?'

'No, I don't think he said. If he did, I don't remember.'

'His name?'

'I almost know,' Marcus said, frowning and tapping his forehead with his knuckles, 'it was the same name as someone famous, a sports person. McEnroe! That's it, like the tennis player. Not a surname you hear every day. Not John, but something similar. Was it James? Not James, I don't think. Jeff? Something like that. A "J" name, at any rate, if I'm not mistaken.'

Sean had reached them with his bounty of plants. 'Look at this haul!' he said, delightedly. 'Let's get them home, shall we?'

'Sure,' said Julia, distracted by thoughts of teachers and bullies and vulnerable young kids. 'Bye, Marcus, thanks for your help.'

'Bye, Mrs Bird, good to meet you. Good luck with the seedlings. Full sun, remember,' he said, walking back to the centre.

. . .

'I see you've been making friends at the garden centre,' Sean said from the driver's seat. He pulled on his seat belt and started the car. They had decided against stopping for a late lunch in favour of a sandwich at home.

Once he had manoeuvred his way out of the busy parking area with its many hazards – gardeners pushing trolleys of plants, incoming shoppers looking for parking, families wandering about, a rooster that must have escaped the little farmyard – Julia told Sean about the odd coincidence of meeting Marcus, and the even odder coincidence of the reporter's visit just weeks before.

'What do you think it means?' Sean asked. 'Do you think there's a connection?'

'I don't know. But I do think that it seems odd that some reporter seeks out one of Ursula's students – a victim to her bullying – and comes asking about her just weeks before she's killed. I think they must be related somehow. I just don't know how.'

She paused, and added quietly: 'Yet.'

15

For the first time that spring, it was warm enough for Julia to take her breakfast at the little iron table in a sheltered corner of the kitchen garden. The sun came in at just the right angle to gently warm her shoulders. It wasn't a particularly enthusiastic sunbeam, so she was wearing a Puffa jacket over her pyjamas, as well as thick socks and her gardening shoes. She had fed the chickens and collected the eggs in her little egg basket, toured the estate with her faithful companion, Jake, and identified just the spot for her lettuce seedlings.

Now her morning tea and her bowl of honey-drizzled oats were in front of her, alongside her iPad.

When they were married, she and Peter had always got the paper delivered through the brass slot on the heavy front door of their London flat, but Julia had recently succumbed to the online subscription for the weekday edition, with the Sunday paper still arriving as a great stack of newsprint. She suspected that Peter wouldn't have gone along with this new development (let alone her eccentric and far-from-stylish early-morning get-up) but that was the thing about ex-husbands. You didn't have to take their opinions or wishes into account. The online paper was more convenient and more environmentally acceptable, and while she occasionally missed the rustle of the 'real thing', she didn't miss the pile of papers awaiting recycling.

Jake was calm after his walk around the garden and his morning treat of a bit of fat and gristle from last night's chop. He lay quietly at her feet, keeping a lazy eye on the birds that insisted on tweeting and squawking in the bushes. Julia opened her iPad and popped a spoon of oats into her mouth. In between bites, she opened her email. Jess's name gave her a little thrill, there amongst the newsletters and bills and reminders and special offers that seemed to fill her inbox.

Hey Mum,

Great to hear. You sound happy, and a bit different.

I feel like we are communicating better now that I'm far away and you are in this new life, without Dad. Very cool about the relationship, hope to meet him. Looks like summer could work.

Please send pic of 007 and Jake, or participate in social media like the rest of the world.

Love

J

Xxx

Okay, so it wasn't exactly a long and detailed missive, but it had a sort of intimacy and honesty that made Julia happy.

She glanced at the rest of the subject lines in the inbox and saw something from the Women's Institute of Berrywick. She opened the email and clicked on a link to: 'Check out our brilliant bakers and their cakes at the Spring Fair!'

It was a gallery of photographs of the cake bakers holding their wares. Julia scanned the page, looking for herself. There she was, looking quite reasonable, she thought. She was still susceptible to vanity, even on the wrong side of sixty, and was grateful to see that there was no weird angle that gave her a treble chin, squint or peculiar expression. She tried to imagine a stranger looking at the picture. They would see a rather nice-looking woman with a warm yet restrained smile, a good haircut, and a fine-looking chocolate cake. Perhaps she should send this picture to Jess, to share a bit of her new life.

Her eyes roamed the rest of the photographs and fell upon that of Ursula, alive and well, holding her magnificent Easter Bunny cake. It gave Julia a funny feeling to know that an hour or two after this photograph was taken, Ursula was dead.

Julia felt as if there should be a sign hidden in the picture, some sort of foreshadowing of the terrible events that were soon to befall Ursula. But Ursula stood square and steady, holding the cake in front of her, her feet planted slightly apart, her legs in their light grey trousers. The yellow jacket was open, the grey polo neck jersey underneath mostly obscured by a knotted scarf, pale, with green and yellow stripes.

Above the scarf was the face Julia had only ever seen in death. There was no fleeting expression of worry, no hidden anguish, nothing like that. Just the rather wooden and mildly irritable expression of someone waiting for the photographer to get on with it and take the picture.

Beneath the picture was a caption: *Our condolences go out to the family and friends of Ursula Benjamin, who sadly passed away soon after this photograph was taken. May she rest in peace.*

Julia closed her email, opened the newspaper app and

scanned the headlines. Honestly, she sometimes wondered why she bothered. She certainly wasn't in the mood today for the Parliamentary spats, a row over agricultural subsidies for duck farmers, the fires in Australia. She couldn't concentrate, her mind wandering back to Ursula Benjamin. She closed the newspaper app.

Who had killed Ursula and why? By all accounts, she hadn't been an easy woman. It seemed she hadn't been well-loved or even particularly well-liked. Her own son didn't speak to her. She'd been a teacher who picked on certain children badly enough to make at least one of them – Marcus – leave the school. Julia was shocked that Ursula had still been teaching in a supposedly good school, despite what was clearly a pattern of abusive behaviour. But that aside, what did it have to do with her death? Could the murderer have been one of her students? Or someone else she had wronged?

Julia had far too many questions, and far too few answers. Time to get dressed and get on with her day. She picked up her iPad and took one last, long look at the picture of Ursula on the still-open tab. Using two fingers, she enlarged the photograph and studied her face in the hope that it would tell her something about the dead woman.

She gave a little gasp, loud enough to make Jake lift his head from his paws.

How had she not seen it before? The scarf! Ursula was wearing a striped scarf in the photograph, but when Julia and Sean had found her, there had been no scarf.

Julia dropped the iPad and picked up her phone. Her heart pounded crazily while it rang and rang on the other side. No answer.

'Damn,' she said, her finger over the red telephone button, ready to end the call.

The ringing stopped, and a voice said, 'Hello, Julia. What's up?'

She sighed with relief. 'Hayley, I need to talk to you about Ursula Benjamin. I think I've found the murder weapon. And possibly...'

'What?'

'And possibly a motive.'

16

'I have to say, this could be an important discovery,' Hayley said, looking up at Julia in grudging appreciation. She lowered her head and peered deeply into the photograph, enlarging it with her fingers for the fourth time, as if hoping for a further revelation. Julia wasn't optimistic about her chances, having tried the same tactic to no avail, but she understood the impulse.

'It makes a certain amount of sense. I need to check in with forensics and see if it's possible, in light of what the injuries show.' With that, Hayley pushed her chair away from her desk, got up and walked to the door. Opening it in one swift movement, she yelled, 'WALTER!' into the corridor at about a thousand decibels, then slammed the door closed again, setting the dozens of Post-it notes that covered her desk and computer monitor quivering in the resulting wind. This wasn't Hayley Gibson's usual manner, thought Julia, and likely signalled sky-high stress levels. In fact, the younger woman did look tired, her eyes rimmed with red. Her white shirt was rumpled, as if it might be on its second day of service.

Hayley sat back down. 'Say this theory is correct and she

was killed with her own scarf. What does it mean?' she asked, more of herself than of Julia.

But Julia answered: 'It wasn't premeditated. It's not as if someone came out, armed with a gun or a knife or whatever, looking to kill her.'

'Right. It was circumstantial. It was a spur of the moment crime. Committed out of rage. Or passion.'

Julia thought a moment, and said, 'That means it's likely someone she knew, wouldn't you say? If they were arguing or talking to each other before it happened?'

The detective nodded. 'Well, as you know, most murders are committed between people who know each other. But yes, it's likely that she knew her killer, and there was some sort of interaction or altercation between them.'

Their back and forth was interrupted by DC Walter Farmer, who flung open the office door and practically skidded in, his face pink and damp with sweat. 'Hello Detective Inspector, sorry Detective Inspector. I popped out for a Coke. Only gone a minute. I heard you called? Oh sorry, Mrs Bird. Hello.'

'It's all right, Walter. Take a breath. There's some new information about the Benjamin murder. I need you to get in touch with the forensics team.'

Hayley explained about the photograph and the missing scarf while Julia forwarded the picture to Walter's phone.

'From what I can see, it looks as if the scarf is silky,' Julia said. 'Either silk or some sort of silky material. Not rough. Just in case that helps.'

Walter nodded and dashed out again, promising his boss that he would, 'Fast track it asap, if not sooner.'

'Where were we?' Hayley said, irritated at the interruption to her thought process, although it was she who had summoned Walter Farmer.

'She probably knew the killer.'

'Right. Husband and son are off the table, as we know.

Rugby alibi. Nothing's turned up in her personal life that would suggest a motive. No evidence of an affair, although Robert did say they had problems in the past. She didn't have much family. Her parents are both dead. She had a sister in Wales who she saw twice a year.'

'She didn't come to the memorial, as far as I know. At least, there was no mention of her.'

'You went to the memorial?' Hayley asked sharply.

'Yes. Sean felt... We wanted to pay our respects. We'd found her, after all.'

Hayley nodded once, as if to indicate that she accepted Julia's point, but only just.

Julia continued, 'Anyway, speaking of the memorial, while I was there I heard something a bit, let's say... Something that might be relevant. Something about Ursula.'

Hayley leaned back and waited, alert.

'She wasn't popular. More than that, she was... disliked, I think.'

'Really? I heard she was a good teacher, and that her students got top marks.'

'She was a good teacher, if you are talking about explaining concepts. And her students did get good marks. But I spoke to one or two of her pupils and they said she had a nasty streak. That she didn't treat all of the pupils well. She was a bully who would take against someone and pick on them. These kids were really damaged by it – some of them, at least.'

Hayley's eyes narrowed at the thought. 'And you met these kids?'

'Young men now, but yes. One of them is in my book club, which is how I heard about it. Dylan was a student of Ursula's, he's the same year as Luke. And by the way, from what I heard, Luke didn't get on with his mother, either.'

'So you think one of her students could have killed her?'

'Well, it's a possibility, although it's a pretty radical response...'

'If Ursula bullied those boys a few years ago, there's no reason to think she's changed her ways,' Hayley said. 'She's probably been doing it forever and was still doing it. That's a lot of bullied kids. You only need one to crack.'

'True, just one or two a year would mean dozens of damaged, angry young people. It's possible one of them took their revenge.' Julia thought of Marcus who, if anyone, had reason to hate Ursula, but who seemed to have successfully moved past his hurt. Not everyone would be able do the same. Quickly, she filled Hayley in on her conversation with Marcus.

'I think it's time for me to speak to the headteacher, see if he has any idea who might be holding a grudge against his star maths teacher,' Hayley said. 'Starting with her ex-pupils. And while he's about it, he might like to tell me why he turned a blind eye and let her continue bullying.'

'I don't understand that at all.'

The new lead and her anger at the school's negligence seemed to have revitalised Hayley. She got to her feet and pulled her jacket from the back of the chair, swinging it over her shoulder and shoving first one arm into a sleeve, then the other. 'I'm going,' she said. 'Thanks for the lead on the scarf. See you around.'

And with that she picked up the little backpack she used as a handbag and was out of the door before Julia was out of her chair.

Julia found her own way out of the office and down the corridor to the door that led from the offices and holding cells into the waiting area. She'd been to the station often enough. The desk sergeant looked disapprovingly at her as she emerged. She seemed to disapprove of Julia generally. Julia was a civilian, after all, and she had no business palling up with the DI, and sticking her nose into police business.

'Goodbye, Sergeant, have a good day. See you again soon, no doubt,' Julia said cheerfully, in order to irritate her further. It was childish, yes, but it was rather satisfying when she saw the sergeant's ever-present scowl deepen in response to her farewell.

'Mrs Bird! Julia!' Walter called after her. Julia stopped, just as she reached the exit. Walter handed her a plastic bag. 'Your shoes. Thank you. We've eliminated their prints, you can have them back.'

'Thanks, Walter. Glad I could help.'

'We've got shoe prints from Dr O'Connor too, and from the police who were there on the scene, so we can discount all those. We've got a reasonable print left, and when it comes to sneakers, the prints are quite distinctive. It'll be helpful if we ever do find a suspect. There's a good possibility we could match his shoe to the print.'

'He?'

Walter looked flustered; he'd said too much. 'Just an assumption; we don't know that. I just thought. The size, it would be really big for a woman. I shouldn't have said, though.'

'Not to worry, Walter. It's between us. But I have a question for you, if I may?'

'Well, I'm not at liberty...' he puffed, suddenly officious.

'It's a general question, not a specific one.'

'Yes, of course,' he said, eager to be of assistance, and to put his indiscretion behind them.

'Strangulation. How hard is it? I mean, do you have to be strong, or know what you're doing, or could anyone do it? Me, for example?'

Walter gave a mildly patronising chuckle. 'I wouldn't put my money on you, Mrs Bird. It's a very forceful movement, even with a scarf or some such. The victim would struggle, of course. I mean, who wouldn't? Try to get away. And you'd have to keep your grip for a good minute or two. It's much easier if you come up behind and have the element of surprise. And of course in this case, the victim was sitting down, too. That would make it a good deal easier for the killer. We assume he was standing behind her. And she was wearing her own murder weapon, so to speak, so that would have taken strength...'

DC Farmer stopped, realising he was once again talking about a case to a civilian. His face reddened and he started to stammer.

'Speaking generally, of course,' Julia said with a smile.

'Generally, yes,' he said, with an exaggerated nodding of his head.

'Thanks for getting the shoes back to me, DC Farmer,' she said. 'And good luck with the scarf, I hope it's useful.'

17

If there was one thing Julia had never been able to bear, it was a niggling mystery in need of explanation. She hated a loose end. An unanswered question. A missing piece of information. As a child, she had found this quite intolerable. 'But it doesn't make sense!' she would wail at her mother in a fury, about one thing or another. She wanted answers and order.

Very likely, while Julia was walking Jake along the river path, DI Hayley Gibson was right this very minute finding missing bits of information and garnering answers. Very likely she had names and ideas and motives. Julia was dying to know what they were.

You are not six years old, she told herself sternly in her dead mother's voice. *Now mind your own business and enjoy your walk.*

She took her own advice, and returned her focus to her immediate surroundings, which were admittedly very lovely. The sky was the colour of an apricot, from a pale creamy yellow on one horizon to a fiery pink on the other, reflecting in silvery waves on the water. The soft light made the whole world seem peaceful and calm.

The usual suspects were out and about in their numbers. She gave a friendly wave to the running woman with the swinging ponytail, and the two clever border collies who trotted obediently at her heels without even a leash. She greeted Yorkie Lady as she passed her with her brace of little dogs. She aimed a friendly nod towards a young couple, clearly tourists, taking photographs of each other leaning against the old bridge in the kind light and sporting wide smiles – for Instagram, Julia suspected.

Jake pulled at his lead, yearning to investigate a particular bush. It looked to Julia like any other bush alongside the path, but he'd found half a hot dog sausage under it months ago and had never forgotten it. 'And people say Labradors aren't clever,' she said, slipping him from his lead. 'But you're an Einstein-level genius when there's food involved, aren't you, Jake?' He darted off in eager anticipation which was bound to be disappointed.

'Talking to yourself,' said old Edna, giving Julia a start. Edna had a talent for appearing silently out of nowhere. 'That's how it starts, but how it ends, nobody knows. Except the nose. The nose knows. Where it goes.'

Edna – or Auntie Edna as most of the villagers under fifty called her – emitted random thoughts and phrases that were clearly gobbledygook, but sometimes sounded almost profound.

'Good evening, Edna. How are you today?'

'Rubbish, that's what. Rubbish, I think you'll find.'

The old lady looked even older and thinner than she had at the Spring Fair, a bundle of sticks wrapped in an assortment of shawls and other drapery. Not for the first time, Julia wondered if Edna should be tottering about the neighbourhood on her own, and so close to water. The inhabitants of Berrywick seemed to think that she was cannier than she looked, and possibly immortal.

'Enjoy your walk then, Edna,' Julia said, moving on to

where Jake was snuffling hopefully for the other half of the sausage.

What would happen now, Julia thought, ignoring her dead mother's instructions and letting her mind return to murder, was that Hayley would spend a few days investigating a list of Ursula's least-favoured pupils. Julia wasn't optimistic about her chances of success by this method. She felt there was a piece of information missing in this equation. It was the timing, she thought. If this bullying had been going on for years, why had Ursula been killed now, and not a year ago, or five years ago? There must have been something else going on to trigger the murder.

Which brought her back to the question – why would a reporter have sought out Marcus Featherstone? This McEnroe fellow had been investigating the bullying *before* Ursula's death. Why?

'Jake!' she called. 'Come on, boy, home time. We've got work to do.'

Back home she poured herself a glass of lemonade, put her laptop onto the table, and got to work. Putting 'McEnroe' into the Google search bar was, of course, a useless exercise. It simply brought up the tennis player. 'McEnroe journalist' brought up a hundred versions of a story in which the tennis player blasted a journalist. She was going to have to work a little harder. She set the search to 'UK results only'. Marcus had said the journalist had a 'J' name. She tried James and Joseph and Joe McEnroe, then Jacob and Jeremy. No luck. She narrowed the date field. She tried Jonathan and, with a smile, Jake. Finally, she tried Jim.

Bullseye.

Jim McEnroe, reporter, the *Southern Times*. There was an email address for him, and a phone number for a tip line, which seemed rather a quaint notion in this day and age. Julia looked at the clock in the corner of her computer screen: 8.30 p.m. She sent a one-line email to Jim McEnroe, asking him to please call her in connection with St Martin's. Hopefully he'd see it first thing in the morning and phone her right away.

Not ten minutes later, as she was peering into the fridge, regarding its contents with some despair, her mobile phone rang. Without even closing the fridge door, the white light still illuminating the sad bits of cheese, wilting lettuce and jars of chutney, Julia turned to the kitchen table and grabbed her phone.

'Julia Bird, hello,' she said to Unknown Number.

'It's Jim McEnroe, *Southern Times*,' came the reply. 'It sounds like we need to meet.'

Julia scanned the tables. Only two had single male diners. One was Johnny Blunt, wearing his inevitable blue knitted cap pulled down to his eyebrows, despite the warm weather. The village had all been pleased when Johnny had only received a suspended sentence for his role in the first murder that Julia had stumbled upon in Berrywick. Johnny was back in his place at the Buttered Scone, but Johnny Blunt was nobody's journalist. The other diner, a long-haired young man tucked into a quiet corner away from the counter, seemed too youthful to be an investigative reporter, but he was scanning the arrivals to the Buttered Scone, and raised a hand to Julia in a tentative wave. She walked over to the table, and he said, 'Mrs Bird? Jim McEnroe.'

'Hello,' she said, sitting down. His phone and a spiral-bound notebook and a pen were on the table. Flo came over and took their orders – just coffee for both of them. It was all business, it seemed. No cream teas today.

'So, your email...' Jim said, cutting straight to the chase. 'How did you find me, and why?'

'I heard from... a friend... that you were making enquiries about bullying by teachers at St Martin's. I have an interest in the story.' Julia didn't want to give away too much before she had heard what he had to say.

'And that is?'

'Circumstances have recently brought me into contact with a couple of past pupils and a teacher. I heard some disturbing stories. I'm a social worker by profession, although I must add that this isn't an official inquiry. And yourself?' It was her turn to ask questions, now.

'Working on a story for the paper,' Jim said. 'I got an anonymous letter alleging ongoing bullying by staff.'

'I see. And this letter, when did it arrive?'

'About two or three weeks ago, I'd have to check.' Jim tucked his long hair behind his ear. Julia was never quite sure how she felt about long hair on men, but it seemed to suit Jim's narrow face.

The letter had arrived well before Ursula's death, which was interesting.

'So you've been talking to past students?' she asked. 'Who did you talk to? What did you find out?'

Jim hesitated. 'Well... Since we're asking questions, I've got one too. You said you came into contact with a teacher. Who was it?'

This dancing around each other wasn't going to work.

'I'll tell you what,' Julia said. 'I'm going to trust you not to quote me or write about what I tell you without consulting me. You can trust me to do the same – I'll keep your info to myself, unless you give me permission to spill the beans, or it's something that the police need to know in the interests of public safety.'

Jim surveyed her thoughtfully, his professional distrust

fighting with his desire to know what she knew. His curiosity won out.

'Right. You've got a deal.'

'The teacher was Ursula Benjamin.'

His eyes shone with excitement for a moment, but he covered it up quickly, slipping back into professional mode. 'I see. The dead woman.'

'Yes. I found her body, and so I have taken an interest in the case. I have been involved in the police investigation. I went to the memorial and met some of the students. One of them told me a journalist had come asking about the bullying at the school. That's it, in a nutshell.'

Julia sat back and waited. She could see that Jim was desperate to hear more, but it was his turn to offer information now. She raised her eyebrows slightly in a questioning gesture. He started to speak.

'As I said, I received an anonymous letter. Handwritten, on actual paper, can you believe? I found it on my desk, with my name on the envelope, like it's 1980. I felt like some boomer actor from an old movie. Anyway, the letter claimed that this bullying had been going on for years. Children had left the school because of it. It referred specifically to Mrs Benjamin as the perpetrator. The letter claimed that there had been complaints, but the head, David Schofield, didn't discipline her in any way. It said, and I'm quoting directly here, "That woman is still there, ruining children's lives. It has to stop." And the writer said it was my duty to investigate and write an exposé.'

Their coffees arrived. Flo hung about for a minute, as if hoping for a chat, but they both thanked her brusquely and she went on her way.

Jim took a sip of coffee, and then continued. 'The last line of the letter is the one that has me lying awake at night, though,' he said.

'What did it say?'

'It said, "If someone doesn't do something about this, I'll get rid of that bitch myself."'

'Gosh,' said Julia. 'That's certainly strong language. And significant, given what happened. So, what did you do?'

'I started tracking down kids who had left the school before finishing, or in mysterious circumstances. Your basic reporter footwork – you find one source, that one gives you another name, and so on.'

'How many have you found so far?'

'Five.'

'Marcus Featherstone being one of them.'

'Yes. Four more. One of them deceased, I'm sorry to say.'

She had to ask. 'Suicide?'

He shook his head. 'No, but it might as well have been. Drugs. I've only been on the story a short while, so it's quite likely that there will be others.'

Julia felt sick and sad at the thought. 'What did the school say? Did you question the headteacher?'

'He's been avoiding me. I left two messages, but he didn't get back to me. And then Mrs Benjamin died, and he emailed to say that the school was in mourning, he didn't have time for interviews but that everything was under control. To please respect their privacy at this difficult time, and so on. He was hedging, basically.' Jim looked grumpy.

'Let's think about the letter,' she said. 'Do you have it on you?'

'No, just a photograph. I left the original in my desk at home. It's evidence, you know.' He pulled out his phone, scrolled to find the picture, and handed it over. 'Here.'

Julia read it once quickly and once slowly, then gave it back, saying, 'It sounds to me like it's written by someone who's still connected to the school.'

'Yes, you're right. I thought so too, or how would they know it's still going on?'

'Could it be another teacher or a teacher's assistant? Support staff, like a secretary or something? A parent?'

'Could even be another student.'

'What about the paper, the envelope? Any clues?'

He shook his head.

Julia reached for the phone again and examined the small image with its four spare lines of loopy writing, and continued with her train of thought: 'What about the handwriting? It doesn't seem like a teenager's writing to me, although I'm no expert. And besides, what teenager would write on paper?'

Jim smacked his hand down on the table and said, 'I should have thought! I've got a cousin who's a graphologist.'

'Graphologist?'

'Handwriting expert. I'll see if she can tell me anything about who wrote it.' He seemed very pleased with himself.

That sounded like a lot of nonsense, quite frankly, but Julia wasn't going to get into that. 'Right, you do that.'

Jim smiled. 'Thanks for helping me think about this,' he said.

'There's something else,' Julia said.

At her serious tone, he looked up from his coffee to meet her eyes.

'We're going to have to tell the police about the letter.'

A look of sulky resentment came over his face, and he started to speak, struggling for the words.

'We have to, Jim. You can't withhold it, not now that there's a murder investigation. I've been speaking to the detective, and I can't not tell her. They know about the bullying situation, it's not new info, but there might be something in the letter that helps the investigation. Especially given the threat at the end.'

Resentment turned to resignation. 'Yeah, you're right. You can tell your detective contact. I'll send you the photo. I can take it around if they need the original – I live nearby.'

'Oh?' said Julia.

'The little yellow cottage over on Melody Avenue,' said Jimmy. 'I inherited it from my Gran.'

'Lovely,' said Julia, who had walked past the cottage and noticed how its unusually coloured walls somehow brought out the best in the cottage's pretty garden. No doubt also the work of Jimmy's late grandmother.

'Anyway, I'd better go, I've got some more leads to follow up. Talk later,' Jimmy said, trying to catch Flo's eye to signal for the bill.

'I'll get it,' said Julia. 'You get back to work.'

'Thanks,' he said, standing up. 'Next one's on me.'

As he turned to go, she had a final question: 'Jim, why was the letter addressed to you? Not to the editor, or anyone else at the paper?'

He looked at her and shook his head. 'I've racked my brains, but I can't say I've had any bright ideas on that one.'

18

On Wednesday morning Julia did something she hadn't done since she'd moved to Berrywick and started volunteering at the charity shop – she phoned to say she would not be at work at Second Chances that day.

She'd been all ready to go to the shop – chickens fed, eggs collected, Jake walked, oats eaten – when she got a call from Hayley Gibson. Her name on Julia's phone screen caused a little fillip of excitement. What had Hayley discovered from Mr Schofield? It wasn't like her to phone Julia and share information, but maybe this time...

Julia answered.

'I need your help,' Hayley said, without so much as a hello, let alone a morsel of interesting new information. Hayley was not a morning person at the best of times, but even from her usual low base of early good cheer, she sounded grumpy.

'What do you need?' Julia said.

'This fellow you spoke about, the one who was bullied. Can you tell me where I can find him?'

'Marcus. He works at the big garden centre on the way to Edgely.'

'Edgely? Damn. I'll have to wait until I can get a car. Mine didn't start properly this morning. It made that noise like a cat about to vomit: *gghhh gghhh gghhh spit spit*. Because I don't have enough irritation lined up for today.'

'Spark plug, perhaps?' Julia was no motor mechanic, but she recognised the *gghhh spit* sound from an annoying car problem of her own. She remembered it as being rather an easy thing to solve, but that might have been because Peter had sorted it out, as always. She felt a little pang at the thought that never more would Peter sort out annoying car problems for her.

'Maybe. Anyway, the guys from the police garage are coming. But can you believe there's no spare at the station?' Hayley said, irritably. 'Walter's trying to find one for me. But you know Walter. Can't organise anything, poor boy.'

'I could drive you,' Julia said, on the spur of the moment. 'There's something I wanted to tell you. Something that might be useful. I was about to phone you actually, but we could talk in the car. Two birds, one stone, you know.'

She waited out the silence, until Hayley sighed and said, 'Okay, thanks. I suppose you might introduce me to Marcus too, seeing as you already know him.'

'Yes, we had a good rapport. I'll be there in twenty minutes,' said Julia, trying to keep the eagerness out of her voice.

She ended the call and immediately rang Wilma, who sounded mildly aggrieved at Julia saying she wouldn't be coming in. Although she warmed up when Julia explained that she had to speak to the police regarding the murder.

'Of course! Goodness, anything that helps find the killer of that poor woman. But why would they think you'd know anything?'

Julia pleaded ignorance, whilst implying that she might know more after today's meeting.

'You go along then, and do keep us posted. We all feel just awful about it,' said Wilma. 'See you next week.'

. . .

Julia picked Hayley up from the police station and started talking, filling Hayley in on what Jim McEnroe had told her. She described the accusations in the letter, the threat and said that Jim would send a picture.

Hayley nodded. 'That's very interesting, Julia. It all ties up with what Marcus told you,' she said. 'A bullying scandal. That won't go down well with Mr Schofield.'

'How *was* Mr Schofield?' asked Julia. She felt that she could cut to the chase, since she was providing the transport, and had shared everything she knew from Jim McEnroe.

'Not very helpful, unfortunately. He didn't deny the bullying allegations, but said they were few and far between and had been dealt with internally and resolved.'

'"Dealt with internally" always sounds like a cop-out, in my experience,' said Julia. 'It's code for, "Didn't want to create a fuss or attract negative attention."'

'Exactly. He looked a bit uncomfortable when he spoke about it too. Then I asked him if there were any current issues and that's when he really clammed up. Said there had been a complaint. From what you've just said about your reporter friend, the complaint might well be related to that, but he couldn't give me the name or any details until he has checked with the lawyers. I didn't expect him to, to be honest. That's what it's like now, protection of personal information and so on. We usually have to get a warrant these days.'

'Yes, it's especially difficult where children are concerned. I've had this problem myself.'

'Right, I'm sure. Must have been a minefield in Youth Services, dealing with minors.'

'Yes, we were very careful to protect their rights and their information.'

'Well, I'm sure you were very meticulous about that, and always did the right thing.'

'Oh, I don't know. I didn't always get things right.' For a

moment, Julia considered confiding in Hayley. Telling her about that last awful case and how very wrong Julia had been. But Hayley had started speaking again.

'Upshot is, I'll have to wait until Schofield has checked with the school's lawyers. That, after fighting my way into the car park at home time. I hadn't realised. I arrived at four. You should have seen the mess. Big cars getting in each other's way. And when I finally got a spot, there were three or four parents waiting for him while I was in the secretary's office. Honestly, they were pacing about. There was one tall tree trunk of a woman who was quite fierce with the poor secretary, said she would wait until midnight to see him if she had to. I felt quite sorry for the man, having to put up with entitled parents all day. The only mildly entertaining thing was to see their faces when the secretary told them that the detective would have to go first and they could all wait. Annoyance, mixed with intrigue.'

'Small victories,' Julia said with a smile.

'I'll take what I can get!' Hayley seemed a bit more relaxed now. 'Although then again, the car broke down on the way back, so that cancelled out any feelings of victory. Anyway, Mr Schofield said that when he gets the go-ahead, he'll tell me everything he knows. In the meantime, I thought I'd follow up on the one name I *did* have – thanks to you. Marcus Featherstone.'

The timing couldn't have been more perfect. As Hayley said his name, Julia indicated right at the giant teacup sign and swung into the car park. It was a lot less busy than it had been on Sunday, but there was a fair smattering of shoppers and cars at ten thirty on a Wednesday morning. The two women got out of the car and crunched across the gravel to the entrance.

'Can I help you?' asked a sunny blonde girl in the garden centre's orange uniform.

'We're actually looking for Marcus,' Julia said. 'He helped

me last time.'

'Oh sure, well, he's not here I'm afraid. He didn't come to work today.'

'Oh dear, I hope he's not ill,' Julia said.

'I don't know. He didn't call. It's very unlike him. He's as reliable as clockwork, is Marcus.'

It was probably just a summer cold. Maybe he'd taken a cold medicine and overslept. So why did Julia feel that dull sense of foreboding in the pit of her stomach? She caught Hayley's eye and saw a look that told her the detective felt the same.

'Anything I can help you with?' asked the girl.

Hayley's phone rang, and she took the call.

'Thank you, but I think we'll just look around,' said Julia, awkwardly, while Hayley barked into the phone.

'Where? Right. Right. Mmmm... Know it. I'm round the corner... On my way. Has someone phoned the coroner's office?'

The girl's eyes grew wide. 'The coroner?' she said. 'Goodness.'

'Come on,' said Hayley to Julia, turning sharply on her heel and heading for the exit at a swift clip.

'Thanks, we'll come by another time,' Julia said, waving awkwardly as she set off after the detective at a pace between a brisk walk and a jog.

'What's going on?' she asked as they reached the car. Hayley was already pulling at the door handle when Julia clicked her remote control. As the doors unlocked Hayley wrenched hers open and got in, pulling her seat belt over her shoulder and buckling it in. Her every movement was fast and efficient, and Julia felt slow by comparison, fumbling the key into the ignition. She turned the car on.

Hayley relaxed a little once they got going, and answered Julia's question. 'There's been a break-in and, it seems, a suspicious death. It's at 134 Nettleleaf Lane, Edgely. It's not far from here. Five minutes. Left here, then right at the roundabout.' She was clearly agitated. 'I shouldn't be taking you to the scene of a crime,' she said. 'But it would be ridiculous for me to go all the way back to Berrywick. Just don't touch anything while we're there, Julia, do you hear me? Just stay outside while I do my job.'

Julia nodded, and concentrated hard, driving faster than she was used to. Her hands gripped the wheel. Hayley sat grim-faced in the passenger seat. It was hard not to jump to conclusions. A reliable man who hadn't turned up at work, and a dead body just down the road. Julia couldn't let herself think about it. Marcus had seemed so full of hope about the future.

Once they turned into Nettleleaf Lane, the house wasn't hard to find. Already, a squad car was parked outside, light flashing, and a couple of uniformed police were keeping nosy neighbours at bay. Julia parked in the road and they got out. The officers recognised Hayley – or Hayley's badge – and waved them into the front garden. Crime scene tape cordoned off the front porch and the front door. The door was open, the windowpane smashed, and broken glass scattered around.

A uniformed officer approached them. 'If you could go around the side of the house, ma'am, you'll find a back door to the kitchen. The officers will show you in. Need to keep this area undisturbed. As you can see, the perpetrator seems to have gained access by breaking the window and opening the door. Forensics are on their way. Follow the path.'

Hayley thanked the officer and followed her pointed finger with its surprisingly shiny and surprisingly purple fingernail.

Then she turned back. 'Wait here, Julia, okay?'

'Will you just come and tell me... you know... if it's Marcus?'

Neither woman had given voice to this fear until now, but Hayley's curt nod told Julia that it had been on Hayley's mind as much as it had hers.

Julia wasn't quite sure what to do with herself. She felt too jumpy to just go and sit in the car, waiting, but she also knew that she couldn't follow Hayley into the crime scene. She stood at the garden gate, looking wistfully up the path that Hayley had taken, when the same uniformed officer approached her.

'Everything okay, ma'am?' He was a young man, with the traces of acne still on his cheeks, and a sad attempt at a moustache shadowing his upper lip. A junior, thought Julia. Perhaps his first murder scene.

'Gosh, yes, I'm fine,' said Julia. 'Just waiting for DI Gibson. But gosh, what a thing, isn't it?'

'Terrible business,' said the young officer. And then, sounding suddenly younger, he added, 'I'm quite shook up.'

'It must be awfully upsetting, seeing something like this,' said Julia, who had no actual idea what the officer had seen.

'It was, ma'am.'

'So,' said Julia. 'What's the working theory?'

The young man was eager to share what he knew, and perhaps make himself seem more important than he was. A common need amongst men his age, as Julia well knew. 'Looks like a robbery gone wrong, ma'am. Our theory is that he thought the house was empty, until he came upon the homeowner in his study. Smashed his head with a golf club. Messy business.'

'Oh dear,' said Julia, picturing Marcus, his head bashed in. She felt quite faint thinking about it. She did hope that Hayley would be out soon, just to tell her one way or another.

'Do you know who he was?' she asked the officer hopefully.

'No, ma'am,' he said. 'But I'm new, so I don't know many people in the village yet. The other officer – the DC inside – he said that...'

But Julia wouldn't ever learn what the DC had said, because Hayley came walking down the path at that moment.

'Julia,' she said, and there was a note of approval, presumably because Julia had stayed exactly where Hayley had left her. 'Julia, I just had to come and tell you. The victim is someone we know.'

19

'It's David Schofield. The headteacher from St Martin's. Looks like he's been dead a few hours,' said Hayley, in her matter-of-fact way.

'David Schofield?'

'Yes.' Hayley's voice became gentler. 'Not... you know. Not anyone else.'

'Right,' said Julia, feeling a bit dizzy. 'Well, that's good. Although not for Mr Schofield of course.'

Hayley nodded. 'Got to get back to the scene. Stay here, Julia,' she warned again, and walked off. The young officer followed.

Julia made her way up the garden path to the steps of the little porch. She sat down heavily, feeling most peculiar. She closed her eyes and concentrated on taking several deep breaths.

'You okay?'

She slowly opened her eyes to see the officer peering down at her. The dizziness that had threatened to pitch her onto the floor had receded to a faint light-headedness, coupled with mild embarrassment. 'I just got such a fright when Hayley said it was someone we knew. Jumped to conclusions.'

'It's a terrible thing, death,' said the officer, as if he was most experienced in the matter. 'You take all the time you need.'

Julia didn't share the exact number of dead bodies she'd seen in the past year – five – with the sergeant. Instead she gave him a weak smile and said, 'I'll just sit here a moment longer if you don't mind.'

'No worries. The forensics guys are finished around in there for now. Dusted the door. Checked for footprints. They've got what they need.'

'Did they find anything interesting?' she asked, because you never knew what someone would tell you, especially when you were a harmless sixty-something lady who'd come over a bit poorly.

'It's not like those police procedurals you see on the telly,' he said with an indulgent chuckle. 'It takes a while to get information. But there was a trainer print, that much I know.'

'Ah, well that's probably useful information,' she said. 'Although everyone wears trainers these days, don't they?'

'Yeah, but more likely to be a younger chap than an older chap, you might say.'

'Yes, you're quite right on that. Or even a woman?'

'Too big, I'd say from the looks of it. Besides, a crime like this, house-breaking, you'd be looking for a man, most likely. Maybe more than one.'

Julia suspected that the young man was simply repeating what he had heard the more experienced police officers say inside the house. 'Well, you'd know best,' she said with a smile.

She turned to look at the front door. 'Tell me, was the front door open like that when you police arrived?'

'Yes, wide open. We haven't touched it. He hadn't even bothered to close it after him when he left. And there was glass everywhere, from the break-in.'

The glass was still there, undisturbed behind the police line, littering the small front porch. Julia looked again, her brain snagging on what she was seeing. She ran through a little movie in her mind. The killer approaching the closed front door, smashing the glass, reaching in to unlock the door and then pushing it open. There wouldn't be any glass outside, surely?

Before Julia could fully think through the scenario, Hayley appeared again, looking grim. Julia took a surreptitious photograph of the front door and the surrounding glass to ponder over later, and turned to the DI, who said, 'You all right?'

'Yes, fine now, thank you,' said Julia. 'Sorry. The shock.'

'Well yes, I can't blame you. It is shocking. He was killed with his own golf club. A hard blow to the temple. Looks like he hit his head on the desk when he fell and snapped his neck.'

Julia's queasiness was coming back at the thought of it. She was about to tell Hayley her observation about the front door, when they were distracted by a small commotion at the gate. A uniform officer waved over to Hayley.

'You okay to walk?' she asked Julia.

'Fine,' said Julia, with more certainty than she felt.

'Come on, then.'

As they walked, Julia took out the photo she had taken of the front door. 'Hayley,' she said. 'Have a look at this. Look which way the glass fell. I don't know if you noticed.'

Hayley stopped in her tracks and took Julia's phone. 'Good Lord,' she said, zooming in on the picture. 'You're quite right. It looks as if the glass was broken after the door was opened. It wasn't a break-in at all, was it?'

'I don't think so,' said Julia. 'I think someone wanted it to look like a break-in.'

'Likely someone he knew. That changes everything,' said Hayley, a note of excitement in her voice. 'Let me go back and chat to the team.'

As she was about to turn, one of the officers – the woman

with the surprising manicure – called from where she was standing on the road, talking to a young woman with a ponytail and tired blue eyes. 'DI Gibson,' called the officer. 'I think you might want to hear this.'

Julia and Hayley headed for the gate, where the officer had been speaking to neighbours.

'What's up? Anything useful?' asked Hayley.

'Looks like it, DI Gibson,' said the officer with the surprising manicure, looking rather pleased with herself. 'This lady might have seen our perp.'

A young woman nodded eagerly. 'That's right. When I left my house to take the children to school there was a young man hanging around. He didn't look like trouble, so I didn't call anyone. He was just sitting across the road, leaning against the low wall at the Sanderson's place, opposite Mr Schofield's. It just looked as if he was waiting for someone.'

'DI Hayley Gibson, thank you for your cooperation. What time was this?'

'It would have been about seven thirty this morning. I was a bit late getting away because my Joe can never locate more than one football boot at any one time, and Alex was eating his oats at a snail's pace. We looked for the boot, and once we found it, and breakfast done with, we left. Their school is almost over in Berrywick and you know what *that's* like – the traffic can be a nightmare, especially if you're a few minutes late.' This was a refrain Julia had heard since she'd moved to Berrywick. It usually meant that you had to wait for a light change on the main road going out of the village, and perhaps slow down for a horse and rider when you neared the stables. 'I feel awful now, of course. But I wasn't really thinking about the chap on the road, to be honest. My mind was on what I'd make for supper. It's a long day, what with football practice, and you know boys, always hungry.'

Hayley gave an understanding tut and a nod, as if she was

well aware of the eating habits of young football-playing boys, although from the little Julia had gathered about Hayley's personal life, she fed only herself and her cat. Julia suspected that most of Hayley's meals were eaten standing up at the kitchen counter or in front of her computer.

'What can you tell us about the young man? What did he look like?'

The woman frowned in concentration. 'If I had to guess, I'd say he was early twenties. Can't say I noticed anything about him except his hair.'

'His hair? What was noticeable about that?'

'Bright red, it was. You don't often see a colour quite like that. Like a flame, or a flower. You couldn't miss it.'

It was well past lunch by the time Julia and Hayley left the crime scene, so they decided to stop at one of the gastro pubs that they'd passed on their way home. Julia chose a sun-dried tomato quiche, and Hayley a steak-and-kidney pie. Once the food had arrived and their appetites slightly sated, the two women couldn't help but go back to discussing the crime.

'I just don't think Marcus Featherstone seems like a murderer.'

'The red hair, Julia.'

'I know. But it could have been someone else. Or he might have been there, but not...'

Hayley shook her head. 'You just showed me the glass,' she said. 'We know the whole break-in story was a set-up, agreed?'

'Yes,' said Julia reluctantly. 'It must've been someone Schofield knew. And just like with Ursula, no premeditation – no weapon brought to the scene. Just grabbed a golf club and hit him. Not even that hard.'

'Exactly,' said Hayley. 'We're looking for an angry young man.' She sounded very sure of herself.

'Okay,' said Julia. 'You're probably right. But that doesn't mean it's Marcus. There were other angry young men.'

'Julia, I know you liked the guy, but it makes some sense. Marcus was bullied at school by Ursula. He killed her.'

'And what about Mr Schofield? Why would Marcus kill him?'

'I don't know. Failure of care? Schofield should have protected the children and got rid of Ursula Benjamin. He didn't. He let her get away with it.'

'True. But why kill him all these years later? Why?'

'There must have been a trigger, something we don't know about. Another piece of the puzzle.'

Julia's phone rang. 'It's Jim McEnroe. The journalist,' she said to Hayley. She took the call and put it on speakerphone. She put her finger to her lips. Hayley nodded her understanding, and took another bite of her pie.

'Hi, Julia. My cousin, the graphologist came back with some thoughts about the writer of the letter,' Jim said. 'Want me to read it?'

'Yes, please do, go ahead.'

Hayley grinned – the first smile Julia had seen from her all day – and rolled her eyes as Jim began to read in a dull tone.

'"The writer appears to be a woman, and she is likely one of the water signs of the zodiac, perhaps even Pisces, as evidenced by the wave-like formation of the letter 'w' and the flow of the sentences towards the margins of the page."'

Jim gave a small cough, which Julia took to be a sign of embarrassment. There was an answering squeak from Hayley. Julia turned to look at her – she was making a wavy motion with her hand and shaking with suppressed laughter.

'"The writer shows signs of distress, even anger, in the determined application of the pen to paper during punctuation."'

Another squeak from Hayley, louder this time, followed by

a snort. Julia felt a surge of hysteria rushing up through her belly to her chest.

Jim continued reading: '"It is likely that the writer is female. An only child, or possibly one of two. Likely vegetarian."'

Hayley made a *gaahh* sound.

'Pardon?' Jim asked.

'Nothing,' Julia said, only just holding herself together. The hysteria had reached her throat.

Jim continued, '"The writer leaves large spaces between their words, which indicates they might be a loner. Dotting the 'i' to the right is a sign of impatience."'

Hayley barked out a sort of choking laugh. The detective inspector had her fist against her mouth and tears rolling down her cheeks. Julia herself was struggling for breath as the waves of silent laughter rolled up inside her, threatening to break free at any moment.

'Is that a dog?' Jim asked, which elicited an actual shriek from Hayley.

'Yes. Dog,' Julia managed to squeeze the words out between spasms. 'Sorry. Bit of a situation here. Call you later.'

She killed the call and the two women gave themselves over to the hysterical laughter they'd been holding in. Julia's little car shook as they heaved and ho-ed and wheezed, slapping their thighs.

'Vegetarian,' Hayley whispered, through tears.

'Impatience,' Julia snorted.

They quietened down, trying to ease their breathing, and then said, at the same time, 'Is that a dog?' which set off another fit of giggles, as well as a bark from Hayley.

Finally, their laughter exhausted, they flipped down the sun visors, and looked in the mirrors to wipe their eyes and remove the tracks of mascara.

'Best laugh I've had in years,' said Julia.

'And I really needed it,' said Hayley. 'I've been in a bit of a funk lately. Had a few things on my mind.'

'If you want to talk about it, I'd be happy to listen,' said Julia.

'Thanks, I appreciate that. And I might take you up on it. But right now, let's go and see if we can find Marcus.'

20

The Featherstones had been easy enough to trace. It wasn't the most common surname, after all. The family home was in central Edgely, not far from the dead headteacher's residence.

Like everyone in the villages, and to Julia's continued surprise, Mrs Featherstone simply opened the door wide at an unexpected knock and gave her unknown visitor a welcoming smile.

Hayley asked if she could speak with Marcus.

'Marcus isn't here, I'm afraid. He is at work,' Mrs Featherstone said. Hayley caught Julia's eye. They both knew that Marcus was not at work.

Mrs Featherstone looked at the visitors with open curiosity, clearly wondering what these two women wanted with her son. 'Can I tell him who came to see him? Or can I give him a message?'

'I'm Detective Inspector Gibson and this is Julia Bird.'

Mrs Featherstone looked flustered, and said primly, 'Well, I'm his mother. What is it in connection with?'

Hayley said that they wanted to talk to him for background information on Ursula Benjamin and St Martin's School. It wasn't exactly a lie, but it wasn't the whole truth either. Hayley hadn't told the woman that her son was the number one suspect in the murder of the headteacher, for a start.

'I haven't been able to reach him,' she explained. 'Could you try and phone him, perhaps, Mrs Featherstone?'

'Of course. Come in. I'll phone him right away.'

They followed her into the entrance hall, where a hefty man hovered. His red hair – faded now – marked him as Marcus's father.

'Ken, they're police. They want to talk to Marcus. It's about St Martin's and Mrs Benjamin. Background information. I'm going to phone him.'

After a gruff greeting, Ken Featherstone led the way into a cosy sitting room, and showed the visitors to two wing-backed chairs. As Julia sat down, a large ginger cat appeared from nowhere, jumped onto her lap and settled down. It was the kind of cat that, despite being of regular proportions, seemed to channel mass from the ether, and pin you down with its weight.

Ken Featherstone sat down on the sofa opposite them and started speaking right away, while his wife searched the flat surfaces for her mobile phone, muttering, 'Where is it now?' under her breath.

'This business with the school. The, um, murder.' He frowned, his weathered face crumpled like a piece of paper in a fist. 'It's upset Marcus, upset all of us. It brought back all these memories. Hasn't been himself, poor boy.'

'A tragic situation. Very difficult for everyone in the school community to lose a teacher so brutally,' said Hayley.

'Not *good* memories,' said Mrs Featherstone, grimly, hauling the phone out from behind a cushion. 'She was his teacher, you know, that Mrs Benjamin.'

'May she rest in peace, Eve,' Ken Featherstone muttered dully.

Eve Featherstone made a harrumphing sound, as if to indicate that she did not share her husband's good wishes for the fate of Ursula Benjamin's immortal soul, and leaned back into the floral sofa that now held the two Featherstones like a big, blowsy herbaceous border. She fiddled with the phone and held it to her ear.

'What was it you wanted to know, exactly, Detective?' Mr Featherstone asked Hayley.

'We're trying to get a picture of what it was like at the school over the years. What Mrs Benjamin was like. We spoke to Dylan Baker. He mentioned that Marcus had been a pupil there, and hadn't been happy. Mrs Bird spoke to Marcus briefly, but I wanted to follow up and ask him more about it.'

'Well, as his father, I can tell you that it wasn't a happy experience. And that was due to Mrs Benjamin.'

'It's ringing,' said Mrs Featherstone.

They all watched her wait and wait. She ended the call. 'No answer. He's at work, must be helping a customer.'

'Could you tell us what happened at school?' asked Julia, gently. 'How did things start to go wrong?'

'When he was in Year Ten, Marcus was put up to the A set in maths. Moved from the Bs, where he was top of the class, to the A, where all the maths boffs were.' Mrs Featherstone looked fleetingly proud at the memory of her son's elevation up the mathematical ranks, but her face clouded over almost immediately. 'He had a good maths brain on him, but he was a nervous boy who needed a bit of encouragement. He got the opposite from that Mrs Benjamin. She took against him. Just didn't like him. Made his life a misery.'

'How awful. In what way?' asked Julia.

'Oh, it was the sort of thing that could be teasing, you know, but mean, and getting the other kids to join in. Like, "We all know which lazybones brought that class average down, don't we?" – that sort of thing. And she called him Wee Marcus, because he's not a big fella, or Agent Orange, because of his hair. It's lovely red, like Ken's.' Mrs Featherstone's voice rose and she was beginning to look quite flushed.

'All a joke, supposedly,' said Mr Featherstone. 'But not funny at all. Not at all.'

Julia hated adults who belittled kids, especially if they rallied the rest of the mob against them. She hated the sound of Mrs Benjamin, frankly.

Poor Mrs Featherstone had abandoned her angry stance somewhat and tears trembled in the corners of her eyes. 'I'm sorry,' she said, reaching into her sleeve for a hankie and then blowing her nose. 'It just got to me, talking about it, even after a few years. It was horrible. I was so worried about him. I'm not a woman with a temper, but that teacher made my blood boil, I can't lie.'

Mr Featherstone patted his wife's hand and picked up the story. 'We found out later that she set these goals, see? To get an average class mark of this or that, to have so many top grades, so many kids getting entry into this or that university. She didn't take kindly to anyone who messed up the class average. That's why she picked on our Marcus. But the more she pushed and prodded and criticised, the worse he got. He lost his nerve.'

'Goodness, where are my manners? I haven't even offered you tea!' Mrs Featherstone jumped to her feet, wiping her face on the clean corner of the hankie, and making a determined effort to recover her composure.

'You're too kind, thank you. But we won't take up too much of your time,' said Hayley, rather to the annoyance of Julia, who was absolutely parched for a cuppa.

'No trouble,' said Mrs Featherstone, getting up from the sofa. 'Ken and I will be having one.'

'A cup of tea would be nice,' said Julia, ignoring a look from Hayley.

'I'll put the kettle on,' said Mr Featherstone.

Eve sat back down and spoke more fiercely once her

husband was clattering in the kitchen. 'The school let Marcus down. We reported the situation to the headmaster, but he was having none of it.'

'The head was Mr Schofield?' Hayley asked.

'Yes. First he said that he would investigate and take action, and we thought it was all going to be fixed. But then, when we followed up, he changed his tune and said he didn't want to interfere. He said Mrs Benjamin was head of the maths department and got excellent results. Refused to even talk to her about her behaviour. It was almost as if he was nervous of her.'

Mr Featherstone came back and fussed about clearing the tea table of the newspaper and pair of reading glasses that it held. His wife went on, 'I think he was scared of losing her. She got the best results in the county. It was even in the papers.'

Mr Featherstone went back to the kitchen and returned with a tea tray. 'Marcus was at that age when things can really go badly for a chap. He lost his nerve, his confidence. Dreaded going to school. We went back to the head. Again, he was no help. He wouldn't hear a word against the teacher. Said Marcus's anxiety was a psychological problem and we should seek help. It wasn't true, even the shrink said. He was fine before... We took Marcus out of the school in the end.'

'I'm sorry, it must have been very hard,' said Julia.

'It was, but he coped,' Mr Featherstone said with some pride. 'Marcus had a bit of a rough time finding his feet after being so badly treated, but he is a brave chap. Got on with it in the end. Got decent marks, got a job. Happy enough. Until now.'

'You mean until Mrs Benjamin's death?' asked Hayley.

His wife nodded. 'That's right. All this talk, and what happened to Mrs Benjamin, it's stirred things up. He hasn't been sleeping well, he's starting to get down. That old anxiety. These last few days I could feel him slipping back to where he was, you know... before. We've been worried, but we've been giving him space, haven't we, Ken?'

'That's right. He's unsettled is all, he'll get over it. He decided to go and talk to Mr Schofield, get it off his chest, say what he had to say. That's what he is going to do. I'm hoping that will clear the air and he'll be better after.'

'I'm not sure it is a good idea, to be honest,' Mrs Featherstone's voice wavered.

'If it's something he feels he's got to do, then he should do it. Get it off his chest. Don't you worry, love. It's going to be all right,' said Ken Featherstone, entirely inaccurately, if Julia's new suspicions were correct.

Hayley breathed deeply, and said: 'Mr Featherstone, Mrs Featherstone, there's something I need to tell you.'

21

Julia was grateful to be in the car and heading home. It had been quite awful, witnessing Hayley tell Marcus's disbelieving parents about Mr Schofield's recent demise, and that Marcus was not, in fact, at work today. And then seeing the unfolding of the realisation that their son, their beloved son, was not just an unfortunate victim of the school's negligence, but – God forbid – a suspect in the headteacher's murder.

For the moment, there had been no mention of his possible involvement in the murder of Ursula Benjamin – after all, there was no evidence there, yet – but it was only a matter of time before his parents joined the dots and considered that for themselves.

But now, the two women were on their way back to Berrywick. Julia was driving. Hayley was on the phone to DC Farmer. From the side of the conversation she could hear, Julia had learned that Walter would start pulling a team together to search for Marcus, and that Hayley's car had been fixed and returned to the station.

'Bloody parents don't have the girlfriend's surname, address or phone number. I ask you, what are people like? So get me a list of people called Milly who live in this area.' There was a pause while Walter spoke. 'Nobody ever said it was supposed to be easy, DC Farmer. Legwork. How many times must I tell you it is all about legwork. And get in touch with the traffic department. See if the cameras have picked up anything useful. It would have been between seven and eight this morning, somewhere around there. Marcus was driving a Panda, red. It's his mum's. I'll message you the reg plate number she gave me.'

Julia was only half listening really. Her mind kept wandering to the time – gone 4 p.m. – and to wondering what dreadful damage Jake had wrought in her long absence. She would be home soon, hopefully while there was still something to salvage from her spring garden. After she had impulsively taken Jake into her home and heart, she had read an article that claimed that chocolate Labs are twenty-four per cent naughtier than golden Labs, and ten per cent thicker. She wondered if Jake was on the standard curve, or whether his figures were more like thirty per cent and twenty per cent. Poor boy, he couldn't help it. It was in his delicious cocoa genes.

While Hayley was messaging Walter, Julia stopped worrying about Jake and began thinking about the things that bothered her about this case; the small threads that didn't tie up. Or did they?

'I've been thinking about how Mr Schofield never did anything about those poor children,' she said to Hayley. 'It's almost like something stopped him. Everyone says that he first acted like he was going to do something, and then became disinterested. It's like someone stopped him.'

'Ursula?'

'I can't see who else,' said Julia, thinking aloud now. 'But how?'

'D'you think she knew something she could threaten him with?' said Hayley. 'Some school scandal?'

'Or some personal one,' said Julia. 'Robert Benjamin

mentioned that he and Ursula had had some marital problem, something that Luke couldn't forgive.'

'An affair?' asked Hayley. 'But with who? She didn't sound like the warmest woman. And how would that tie up with her threatening him?'

'What if the affair was with David Schofield?' said Julia. 'And then she threatened to tell his wife. And that's why he never took action against her.'

'Was he married?' Hayley frowned, obviously thinking about the distinct lack of a wife at the house.

'She died,' said Julia. 'Six months ago. He mentioned it at Ursula's memorial.'

'This is fascinating speculation,' said Hayley. 'But given that they're both dead, and Robert Benjamin has an airtight alibi, it doesn't take us further. They can't have murdered each other, exactly.'

'But it makes the pieces fit a bit better,' said Julia. 'If I'm right.'

'Perhaps,' said Hayley, and then asked, 'Would you drop me at the station? The car's fixed.'

'No problem. I've got to stop at the shops anyway. Tabitha is coming for supper and there's nothing but eggs in the house. Eggs, and half an onion. I thought I'd pick up a few things and make a curry.'

'That sounds very pleasant.'

'Why don't you join us? You'd be very welcome.'

'Thanks, but I'm wiped out after today. I do need to do something about my social life, though. The biggest outing on my calendar is to the Berrywick Residents' Association quarterly meeting next Saturday. I am the official representative of county law enforcement.'

'Maybe if you didn't work so hard you'd have more time for a social life,' Julia said lightly.

'Ah, I could join a pub quiz team like I've always wanted to, but who would want to miss out on the Berrywick Residents' Association quarterly meeting? I've just checked the agenda on my phone and oh, the delights ahead!'

'Like what?' Julia asked, with genuine eagerness. She was still new enough to the village to love the strange little quirks of village life, and the delights of this meeting sounded promising.

'Well, there are the perennial favourites, mostly related to dogs – dog poo, and the picking up thereof, dogs on leads, dogs off leads, dogs barking, lost dogs, dogs chasing cats, dogs chasing dogs, dogs chasing birds, dogs chasing the postman, and so on.'

'I can imagine.' Julia thought about Jake, and his habit of occasionally chasing the ducks. And swans. And pigeons. And wigeons. She hoped he wouldn't turn up on the agenda of the Berrywick Residents' Association meeting.

'In addition, on the agenda next week, we will be discussing the dustbins of Berrywick. Apparently, someone has been messing with them.'

'Oh, that'll be Edna.'

Hayley turned to her in astonishment. 'Edna who?'

'Edna, the old lady. Wandering Auntie Edna.'

'Oh, her. Yes, I've seen her about, of course. She walks along the river path most afternoons.'

'Yes. That's her. Regular as clockwork, is Edna. Always the same route, from what I can see.'

'And how do you know she's been messing with the dustbins?'

'I overheard in the Buttered Scone that she'd taken someone's wine bottles out of their rubbish bin and set them up like skittles in the road. Apparently there were a fair number of bottles. It was a minor scandal.'

'I'll bet!' Hayley laughed. 'I'm surprised I wasn't called out. This is the kind of outrage that usually gets the phone ringing.'

'Well, she's your chief suspect, if you ask me.'

'Well thank you, Detective Julia Bird, for identifying the

suspect. Although quite what I'm supposed to do about it, I don't know. Have a word, I suppose.' Hayley sighed, as if the very thought of having a word exhausted her.

Julia pulled up outside the police station. Hayley opened the car door, and turned to Julia. 'Thanks for all the driving. I'm sorry it all took so long – it was supposed to be a quick drop off and I've kept you all day. I hope it didn't put you out too much.'

'No trouble at all.'

'Good. Enjoy your curry with Tabitha,' Hayley said, and got out of the car.

'Get an early night!' Julia called after her.

As usual, Tabitha arrived with lovely treats, chief amongst them a huge blowsy rose that filled the whole kitchen with its heavy scent.

'From my garden, isn't it grand?' she said.

'Magnificent,' Julia said, gently touching the thick, butter-coloured petals with her fingertip as if stroking a young child's soft cheek.

'And here are some courgettes.' Tabitha's bracelets jingled as she took four fine young marrows out of her basket. 'Not mine, from my next-door neighbour. She's got so many, she can't eat them all. So every time I leave the house, I come home to find she's put another few on my doorstep. I'm just spreading the luuurve.'

'And here's something for you,' Julia said, holding out an egg box with six of her hens' shiny brown eggs lined up in it. She popped it into the basket that the courgettes and rose had come out of, pleased to be able to contribute to this neighbourly exchange of produce and friendship.

Julia poured them each a glass of wine and they sat down for what they had referred to since their student days as a 'debriefing' – a rundown of the important headlines in each woman's life. Tabitha started with an update on her mum's hip replacement, which had gone well, despite the woman's age. Her younger daughter, Tabitha's sister Luanne, was with her. Tabitha would take a couple of days' leave in a week or so, and take over for a bit. The two women agreed that it was a relief to have it over with, and that those ops were very successful these days, and that Gladys was an absolute marvel and would likely be up and about and itching to visit before long.

'And what about you? What's been happening?'

Julia had an entire murder investigation to impart, but instead raised the subject closest to her heart. 'It looks like Jess is coming home. For a visit.'

'That's wonderful news!' Tabitha beamed, but her smile faltered when she saw Julia's face. 'What's the matter? Why do you look so worried?'

'Oh, I don't know. It's just... I've been thinking about parents and children and how we get so much so wrong.'

'Well, that's the truth. There are no perfect parents, that's for sure, but you love that girl and you've done good by her.'

'I was thinking of Ursula Benjamin, too. It turns out that her own son didn't come and visit her when he came all the way to England to visit his dad. I mean, why? What was her side of the story?'

'You are not Ursula Benjamin, Julia. You and Jess always had a great relationship. Yes, when you and Peter split up, it wasn't easy for her. Maybe she wasn't turning her back on you. Maybe she was strong and smart enough to know she needed to go away for a while.'

It struck Julia, not for the first time, that in their relationship Tabitha was the calm, sensible, intuitive one – you'd have thought she was the social worker. When they were together, it was the only time Julia could be the uncertain, frightened, guilty person in the room, instead of the capable, no-nonsense person.

'I don't know. I mean, I guess you could see it that way.'

'You could. You could say you brought up a girl with that kind of insight, and you gave her the space to do what she needed. And that she now feels ready to take the next step back towards you.'

Julia put her hand on Tabitha's forearm and said simply, 'Thank you.'

Tabitha nodded. 'Or you could say it was the thought of living with only your cooking that drove her off. Although you've improved, haven't you? Whatever is in that pot smells amazing.'

'Vegetable curry,' Julia said, getting up to stir the pot bubbling gently on the stove. Admittedly, it was a store-bought cook-in sauce to which Julia had added chopped vegetables, so it was only home-made-ish, but even so. 'And yes, I'm making progress with the cooking. At least if Jess comes back to visit she'll have scones for tea.'

'A major breakthrough in your parenting, I'd say. Could be the saviour of the relationship.'

Julia lifted the lid and lowered her head to smell the curry, and to hide the prickling tears that had come from nowhere. The steam rose in a warm fug, carrying the fragrant smell of ginger and garlic, cumin and cinnamon. She pulled herself together and dipped a spoon into the basmati rice. She brought a few grains to her mouth and tested them with her teeth. Their little hard centres told her they needed another minute. She replaced the lid, turned the rice down low, and turned to her friend. 'Tabitha, can I talk to you about something?'

Tabitha looked at Julia in surprise at her tentativeness. 'Of course, my dear. What is it?'

'I never told you the full story about why I left Youth Services.'

'Well, why don't you do that, then?' Tabitha said with a gentle smile. 'I'm here, aren't I?'

'It wasn't just retirement. There was... an incident. At work. I made a mistake.'

Tabitha, her oldest friend, waited. Julia sat down, and started to speak.

'There was a family. Three children: one girl of ten or eleven, and two little boys. No dad on the scene. In fact, it was the school who first contacted us, worried about the boys. They were missing a lot of school for no real reason, didn't seem to be well-cared for.'

Jake, with his canine sense of humans in need, lumbered sleepily over to Julia and flopped down beside her, his big warm head resting on her feet.

'One of the case workers paid a visit. The mom was in a rough way. Working intermittently, not enough money to go around. Clearly stressed by the kids, who, honestly, were pretty wild. Betty, the case worker, helped her access some services. Did what she could. Kept an eye. The mom was fragile, but seemed to be coping. This went on for a year or so, and then we started getting complaints from the neighbours. Two or three different people. I went with Betty to visit the family. I met the woman for myself. She was fragile, seemed a bit fraught, but she was keeping it together. Only just. Said the kids were exhausting. The girl was hitting her teens. The boys were a handful. As we were heading for our car, a neighbour came out, said the kids weren't safe. Another fellow was hanging around, had the same story. He took my card. Insisted.'

'It sounds serious.'

'It was. I mean, multiple complaints. First the school, then the neighbours. The neighbour phoned a couple of times, with general sort of complaints. Betty followed up. Then on one visit the girl spoke to Betty privately, the daughter. Said her mum was abusive.'

'Ah, no. That poor girl.' Tabitha shook her head. 'What did you do?'

'I couldn't leave them there. I said to Betty, it's time. We need to start the process of getting the children into care.'

'It sounds like you did the right thing for the family.' Tabitha got up, turned off the curry and the rice, and sat back down.

Julia sniffed back tears, wiping her eyes on the sleeve of the velvet jacket that was more like a dressing gown that she wore about the house when the temperature dipped and no visitors were expected. Tabitha being a different matter, of course. 'Well that's just the thing. It wasn't the right thing at all. The mum was on the edge, but she loved those kids and was coping okay. The neighbours had mounted a campaign against her. Wanted them out. I guess the kids were noisy, the little boys running up and down the passages. And the daughter was just having some awful adolescent meltdown and wanted to punish her mother. That poor woman was only just keeping things together, and her awful neighbours victimised her. And I helped them. I tried to take her children away.'

'Ah, love. You weren't to know. You followed procedure. You were misled.'

'Her screaming, when we told her we were going to take those children. I'll never forget it.' Julia started to cry, which sent Jake into such a state that he tried to sit on her lap.

'It's okay, Jakey,' she said, patting his head, and removing his front legs from her thighs. 'I'm all right.'

'What happened in the end?' Tabitha asked.

'Thank heavens, we unravelled it all before we removed the children, but it was close. We helped her with services, and a different place to live. But I still have nightmares about what I did to that woman. The pain I caused her. It was that that made me retire, in the end. I couldn't stand the thought of it, the responsibility for other people's lives. And what I almost did to that family.'

Tabitha got up and came over to Julia, placing her arm

around her shoulder as she sat in the kitchen chair, bereft. 'Ah, lamb, you did your best. The children are all right. And the mum got the help she needed. You did your job.'

Julia leaned against her friend, and the tiny woman felt like a solid rock of love and support. Her dog was at her other side, demonstrating that although he had failed guide dog school, he was his own sort of service animal.

'I keep thinking of it now, with everyone talking about what a bully Ursula Benjamin was,' said Julia. 'How easy it is to make accusations against a person, but how do we know when they are true? What if the accusations are actually just coming from people with their own agenda?'

'I'm sure you'll figure it all out,' said Tabitha, who clearly had no idea what Julia was talking about. 'You're awfully clever about people, Julia. You figured it out about those kids before you did any harm, and you'll figure this one out, too.'

'Thank you. Thank you for listening. I feel better.'

'And you know what'll make us feel better still? A good big bowl of that curry. Come on then, Julia. Let's eat.'

22

Julia woke to the sound of Jake's scratching on the door. Through bleary eyes she looked at her bedside clock and was amazed to discover that it was nearly eight. She couldn't remember when she'd last had nine solid hours of uninterrupted sleep. Before Jess was born, probably. It was her unscientific opinion that once you've slept with one ear open for the sound of a baby, you never quite get over it. It's the end of your trouble-free sleep for life.

She wasn't one for too much psychological reflection, but she felt sure that sharing her story with Tabitha had lightened her spirit and allowed her to sleep the sleep of the dead. All these converging stories of youthful angst – Marcus, Dylan, Jess – had unsettled her and brought up her past failure, but she felt calmer this morning.

'I don't suppose you'd like an amble, young fellow? Take a turn around the place?' she said, opening the door to Jake. For reasons she couldn't explain, she sometimes spoke to him in peculiar voices, as if channelling characters from an old pantomime. He didn't seem to notice – he responded equally enthusiastically to all of them – but it amused her.

He raced around, skidding on the rugs and knocking things over until Julia called him outside and shut the door on him, catching a glimpse of his offended face as she did so. She put the kettle on to boil while she got dressed for the walk. Although it was officially spring, it was nippy out in the mornings, requiring a couple of layers. Speaking of layers, she would collect the eggs and feed the chickens quickly while her tea steeped, and then go straight out once she'd drunk it. Jake's eager whining and scratching was too much to bear for long.

Ten minutes later they were out of the gate and heading down to the footpath along the river. It was their everyday walk. There were others that were longer, or different, or more dramatic, but this one was on their doorstep and it was beautiful: a mix of water views, green verges, weeping willows, occasional houseboats, and charming Cotswold cottages. At this time of year, the riverbanks were dotted with daffodils, their sunny heads bobbing in the breeze.

Having checked the immediate area for fowls, Julia let Jake off the lead to sniff and run. She kept up a brisk pace, while he did about three times her distance, running to the water's edge and back to her, then off to greet another dog, then over to the bench in the hope of a dropped crust of sandwich. It was pleasantly convivial, seeing the same walkers and dogs day after day, the morning walkers and the evening ones, the fast and slow. Likewise, the dogs big and small, the polite and the manic, the fluffy and the glossy.

Their path also crossed with Edna's daily walk, of course, and they'd no sooner set off than Edna's distinctive figure tottered towards them in her usual arrangement of scarves and shawls. She looked somewhere between a dishevelled wanderer and an ageing glamour queen. More of the latter when she tossed one scarf languidly over her shoulder, and said, as she passed Julia, 'Isn't spring the most marvellous of seasons?'

'Morning, Edna,' Julia said. 'Yes, it certainly is marvellous.'

'What is?' Edna said.

'Um, spring?'

'What about it?'

'Well, it's marvellous,' said Julia, feeling like she was the one who was going batty.

'Well I'm not sure about that at all,' came the grumpy reply.

Jake came bounding up and Julia grabbed him before he could upend the old lady, who was unsteady on her feet at the best of times. She clipped his lead onto his collar and told him to sit and stay.

'Sit and stay!' said Edna. 'That's what they say. Sit and stay. Rain, rain go away.'

'Good boy,' Julia muttered to Jake.

'Good boy,' Edna muttered to an empty space by her feet. 'You're a good dog.' She reached into her nest of scarves and pulled out a long, thin striped one. 'On the lead. Whenever you please. Good boy.' The old lady smiled at her imaginary dog, on its imaginary lead. 'No trouble at all.'

That was true enough. The imaginary dog was no trouble, being, as it was, not there at all. The scarf – that imaginary lead – dangled at Edna's leg, its green and yellow the exact colour of the spring daffodils.

It looked familiar, with its green and yellow stripes fluttering in the breeze. Had Julia once had one like it? No, that wasn't it. Seen one in the charity shop?

A jolt of recognition hit her.

Ursula Benjamin. Ursula had been wearing just such a scarf in the photograph taken of her with her cake, minutes before her violent death. If Julia was right, that scarf could be both a clue and the murder weapon.

'That's a pretty scarf, Edna,' said Julia, keeping her tone light and casual. 'Is it new?'

'A gift. Spring sprung from the rubbish like a daffodil. Didn't belong to anyone. Wandered lonely as a cloud, it did, before I found it.' She gave a cackle at her own weird Wordsworthian joke. 'Tossed away. Thrown away like the throne. Like the queen's chair. The dog likes it, now. Don't you, boy?' They both stared down at the absent dog at the end of the dangling scarf. 'Good chap,' Edna said affectionately. Even Jake looked confused.

'Do you remember where you found it?' Julia asked, hopelessly, for Edna was not one to answer a direct question with anything intelligible.

'Of course I do,' she snapped, sharp as a whip. 'What do you take me for? Now good day to you.' And with that, she turned heel and walked away, slapping her bony hand against her thigh and calling her dog to follow her. Her muttering disappeared into the distance, 'Home time boy, good god. Dog. God.'

As soon as she got home, Julia phoned Hayley to tell her that she thought she'd found Ursula Benjamin's missing scarf. And potentially the murder weapon.

'Assuming it's the same scarf, of course,' Julia added, once she'd told her story.

'We asked Robert about that scarf once you'd spotted it in the photograph,' Hayley said. 'They bought it on holiday in France three years ago, at a small boutique. We followed up with the boutique and it was an extremely limited edition scarf. I mean, who even knew that scarves could be limited editions? But there you have it. It's unlikely that anyone in Berrywick would have the same one.'

'And even less likely that someone would be Edna.'

'And you say that Edna is totally batty?' said Hayley.

'Not a term I'd use.'

'Well, she's the one going through the bins?'

'The very same,' said Julia. 'She seems to have moments of lucidity, but few and far between, and they never last.'

'It had to be Edna who had the scarf, didn't it?' Hayley said with a sigh. 'I mean, couldn't it just have been someone I could interview? Some ordinary person who would answer my questions?'

'I'm sorry. Edna has the scarf. You'll have to speak to Edna.'

'Right. I'll try.' Hayley's voice spoke of great reluctance. 'But how does this all tie up?'

'Whoever killed Ursula Benjamin took the scarf. And at some point, they ditched it.' This seemed pretty obvious to Julia.

'Yes, except that I'm pretty sure that Marcus killed Mr Schofield, and my working hypothesis is that he killed Ursula too. There surely can't be two people out there killing the staff of St Martin's School. So how did Marcus get the scarf to Edna? Or how did Edna get the scarf from Marcus? And why?'

'I think she got it out of the rubbish, if that helps you at all,' said Julia. 'On one of her rubbish rummaging outings.' Julia was still struggling to believe that the nice young man she'd met at the garden centre was really a murderer, but she didn't share that with Hayley.

'What makes you say that?'

'She said something about spring springing from the rubbish like a daffodil. The whole sentence might be meaningless, of course. Or – hear me out here – the murderer might have thrown away the scarf...'

'...And in a strange twist of fate, Edna found it.'

'Exactly. Only it's not so strange, I suppose, because we do know that she's been terrorising the dustbins of the good citizens of Berrywick.'

'Yes, I'm going to face the music on that one on Saturday night, remember? At a special meeting of the Berrywick Residents' Association. In punishment for some awful thing I did in a previous existence, no doubt.'

'This doesn't make sense,' said Julia.

'You can say that again. It's completely mad.' Hayley sounded exasperated.

'Indeed, but more specifically, Marcus lives in Edgely with his parents. Edna found the scarf – if I'm right in thinking that's what happened – in Berrywick. She's very much a local rubbish rummager, and she could never have made it all the way to Edgely.' Julia was pleased that this realisation made it seem less likely that Marcus was the murderer.

There was silence on the line as they pondered the various options.

'Well, if I was going to dump a murder weapon slash evidence, I'd likely do it in the next town over, rather than on my own doorstep, wouldn't you?' said Hayley.

'Yes, that's probably true,' Julia conceded. Then she was struck by a brilliant idea. 'Hayley, you should ask who has had their rubbish messed with! Make a list. We might find out who had the scarf in their bin.'

There was a pause as Hayley considered the idea. 'And we might find a connection to Marcus. And perhaps even Marcus himself,' she said slowly. 'That might, in fact, be a not-so-rubbish idea, Julia. Not rubbish at all.'

'But if you think about it, Marcus...'

'Hang on a sec, Walter is waving at me like an insane semaphore operator. What is it, Walter?'

There was some unintelligible low masculine mumbling, and Hayley came back on the line: 'They've got news on Marcus from the traffic cameras at the junction near the crime scene. Marcus has disappeared, still not answering his phone. Hope this'll point us in the right direction.'

And the line went dead.

23

Marcus's mother's red Panda had been picked up on the camera at the junction on the road from the Schofield house early the previous morning, according to Walter Farmer, who was sitting at Julia's outside table enjoying an afternoon cuppa in the spring sunshine.

Julia had spotted Walter when she'd popped up to the shops for some food for supper. Walking past the Buttered Scone, she'd found herself engulfed in a human wave being disgorged from a big blue bus. The wave was German, it seemed, to judge by the occasional guttural phrase she heard over the hissing of the bus. Also, not young, to judge by the grey hair and sensible, sturdy footwear.

In the middle of the wave – the front end of the wave had already poured into the café – bobbed the unlikely head of DC Farmer.

'Mrs Bird,' he'd said, spotting her up against the wall where she was waiting for a gap. He slipped out of the crush and stood next to her.

'Please, call me Julia.' She smiled at him. 'Busy day at the Buttered Scone.'

'Well, I hope you're not looking to get a table. Flo says there's not a seat,' he said, a tad grumpy. 'I haven't had a thing to eat since breakfast. I tell you, Mrs Bird... I mean, Julia... it's been all go-go-go down at the station. Running around looking for Marcus, and heaven knows what else. Quite faint, I am, with hunger. Now that my shift is over, I was hoping for a bit of a sit-down with a cream scone and a nice cup of tea. I suppose I'll just have to get something from the garage shop.'

Julia had heard nothing from Hayley after their conversation had been cut off, and she wasn't expecting to. But DC Farmer might have some news for her. It seemed to Julia that she was presented with both the chance to do a good deed, and find out more about the case.

'I'll tell you what, Walter. I've got fresh scones at home, and some cream,' she said. 'Would you like to come and have some scones and tea with me?'

Walter's face brightened at the thought of scones and tea, but he hesitated, 'Oh, well. If you're sure it's no bother?'

'No bother at all. Come along.'

Julia had warmed up a few of the scones she'd frozen from the last batch she had baked, and DC Farmer was chomping his way solemnly through his second one, dripping with jam and cream and butter. He was one of those slim-built young men who could eat cream scones for every meal and not show it. Not like, say, a sixty-something-year-old woman, Julia thought, waving away his offer of the last scone.

'Please, Walter, you have it. You'd be doing me a favour.'

Walter did his best to look reluctant. 'Well, in that case...' He reached for the butter, and continued: 'So, after the news that the shoe prints match, there was the whole excitement about the cameras.'

He had told her, as they'd walked from the Buttered Scone

to her house, that the forensics had come back and the footprint found in the maze matched a footprint found in Mr Schofield's garden. 'Size ten trainers. Same shoe at both scenes. It's amazing what these chaps can tell about a crime scene, isn't it, Mrs Bird... I mean, Julia?'

Now that they were at Julia's house, he had moved on to the news from the traffic cameras.

'It's frustrating,' he said, continuing his story while moving the knife slowly and carefully, distributing the butter evenly to each edge of the last scone. 'The camera at the junction of the roads to Berrywick, Edgely and Hayfield picked him up at about nine fifteen yesterday morning. Do you know the place?'

'I think so, but I can't picture it. I'm not often out that way.'

'It's a three-way junction. Anyway, we see him driving from the direction of Mr Schofield's house towards the junction. Just as the car is almost out of sight, it stops for a while. God knows why.'

'Traffic?' suggested Julia.

'But there'd been no cars in front of him,' said Walter. 'And he stops for longer than would be normal for a small traffic delay. That's what DI Gibson says.' There was a note of deep respect in Walter's voice when he referred to Hayley. 'Then he moves on.'

'Which exit did he take?'

'That's just it. Whoever decided that the junction was a good place for a camera didn't think that you might need to see which turn-off a car took, not just the fact of them approaching the junction. And wouldn't you know – no other traffic cameras anywhere in the area.'

'How frustrating,' said Julia. 'No way of knowing which turn he took or where he was headed.'

Something was niggling at her, but in the nature of the best – or worst – of niggles, she had no idea what it was.

'You can see he's upset though,' said Walter. 'As he comes

towards the camera. The tech guys could zoom the picture in and he looks like he's crying.' Walter said this with satisfaction. 'He's wiping his face with a hankie.'

'Still, that doesn't mean he killed anyone,' said Julia. 'He could be doing any manner of thing.'

'Like what?'

'Maybe he was crying because of something else completely. Football results. Pet died. Or it could be hay fever.' Julia had to admit that her suggestions didn't sound very convincing, but she hoped there was a reasonable explanation.

'He's less than a mile from the headteacher's house at around the time the man was killed.' Walter popped the last jammy crumb of scone into his mouth and sat back, resting his hands on his tummy with a satisfied sigh. 'You make a fine scone, Mrs B,' he said. 'A fine scone.'

'Well thank you, Walter.' She was, in fact, genuinely flattered by the compliment. The perfection of the scone had been one of the key achievements of her new life in Berrywick.

'I'd best be on my way; the missus will be wondering where I've got to.' As Walter said this, he glanced at his watch and his face clouded with worry. 'Goodness, is that the time? I should really be going. Didn't mean to overstay my welcome.'

'Well, I didn't mean to keep you for so long. Not your fault at all,' Julia said.

Walter nodded, as they silently agreed not to mention the scone-fest beyond the confines of Julia's little garden. And then he was up and out the gate, a little happier and heavier than when he'd arrived.

Julia couldn't settle after Walter Farmer left. She tried to read her novel in the sunny spot on her couch, but she couldn't concentrate on the page. The words danced around while her head buzzed with everything DC Farmer had said. She tried to picture the little car, Marcus's worried face. She wondered about the unexplained stop. She couldn't help feeling that if she could just see the junction for herself, it might all seem clearer. But to go there just to check things out, well, that would surely be the sort of overstepping that Hayley tended to frown at. And Julia did hate upsetting Hayley, of whom she was growing very fond.

'Still,' she said, putting the novel aside and sitting up properly. 'If I were to just find myself there, how could she object?' She looked at Jake. 'After all, we've been wanting to try out the walk around the castle ruins up near Hayfield, haven't we, Jake?'

Jake looked up, and seemed to nod. This was most likely in response to the word 'walk'.

'Well, that decides it then,' said Julia, only mildly concerned that she was having a fully-fledged conversation with her dog. 'If you want to go and walk near Hayfield, who am I to question you? And if the drive happens to take us through the big village junction, well, that's just chance, isn't it?'

At the second mention of 'walk', Jake had stood up and was wagging his tail.

Before she could second guess herself, Julia had Jake's lead and harness on him, and the two of them were in her car and off in the direction of Hayfield and Edgely.

Julia slowed the car as they approached the junction between the three villages. Four roads converged here. Julia's road from Berrywick was one. If she turned left, she would head towards Edgely, and Mr Schofield's house; if she turned right, she would head to Hayfield. The road straight ahead led into one of the upmarket housing estates that were starting to spring up in the area around the golf course. This one – Fairweather Equestrian and Golfing Estate – seemed more upmarket than most. It boasted a large wrought-iron gate with a small guard house next to it. It struck Julia as pretentious and completely unnecessary, but clearly not everyone agreed. A tasteful billboard advised the interested reader that only two units were still available.

Marcus's car would have been heading away from Edgely and the head's house. The question was, had he turned towards Berrywick, or headed straight on to Hayfield? Of course, whichever way he'd turned, he might have gone right through that village and further. But knowing which road he took would perhaps be a start. Wanting to have a bit of a better look, and see if she could work out where the traffic camera was, Julia decided to drive straight on, and park in the little space outside the entrance to Fairweather Equestrian and Golfing Estate. Surely, she thought, as she parked, the balls would bother the horses, or the horses would bother the golfers? What possessed someone to try to combine the two?

She parked her car and, ignoring a hurt glare from Jake, climbed out and looked around. Berrywick or Hayfield? Hayfield or Berrywick? Where had Marcus gone? Of course, she had no way of knowing. The outing was a waste of time. And it was nearly four; she had better get moving if she and Jake were going to get their castle walk. And then there was the weather. Julia glanced up at the clouds to determine the level of rain threat – and then she saw something else, something that gave her a little thrill. On a pole next to the gate, a brace of CCTV cameras surveyed the area. And one of them pointed straight at the junction where just yesterday morning Marcus Feathersone had made his choice. Berrywick or Hayfield? Hayfield or Berrywick? The camera would know.

Julia phoned Walter. He had to get out there and get a look at whatever that camera had seen that morning. The phone rang and rang, and then went to voicemail. She didn't leave a message. No one seemed to listen to their voice messages any more. Instead, she typed:

Call me about Marcus. Had an idea.

She waited a moment or two, hoping he'd call before she got in the car. Nothing. 'Okay, Jake, let's go,' she said, opening the car door.

'Can I help you?' The young man who appeared behind her was presumably the estate security chap, despite being about eighteen years old. He was wearing a navy uniform and a gormless expression. Jake took a great fancy to him, and leaped over from the back onto Julia's seat and out of the door. He fell upon the fellow like a long-lost lover.

'Oh, hello, good boy!' the man said, squatting down to talk to him and stroke his silky ears. 'I've got one just like you. Chocolate Lab. Not as good as you, though. My Jake's a terror.'

'Your dog's called Jake?' Julia asked.

'Yes. Lovely chap, but my goodness, you should see the mischief he gets up to.'

'You won't believe this, but this chap is called Jake, and he gets up to untold mischief too!'

'No!'

'Yes!'

'Well I never. I'm sorry, Mrs... Um...?'

'Bird.'

'Mrs Bird. I know I should recognise you but I'm new. Just started on Monday. My name's Ned.'

Why would he recognise her? Unless he thought he was a resident...

'No need to apologise, Ned,' she said, an idea forming in her head. 'Ned, I wonder if you could help me with something. I got into a little bumper-bashing yesterday at the junction. Some idiot knocked me and then drove off without stopping, can you believe it?' In case she hadn't quite moved him, she added, 'Jake was in the car.'

'Honestly. People today! What is the world coming to?'

Ned looked genuinely shocked and distressed at the appalling low to which humanity had stooped, that a person would not exchange numbers in the event of a traffic incident. Especially when a chocolate Labrador was involved.

'It was a small scrape,' Julia said, hoping he would not look too closely at her car, which did not exhibit the small scrape she claimed. 'But you know, with insurance and so on... I was wondering, would you be able to look at the security footage for me? See if you can see the other car? It was yesterday morning at nine fifteen or thereabouts.'

'I don't know, Mrs Bird...'

She waited. Julia Bird knew the power of letting a moment build.

'I suppose with you being a resident, there's no harm in it, it's just that I'm not very good at computers.'

'I'm sure we could work it out together, Ned. Shall we have a try?' she said with a bright smile.

Minutes later the three of them – Jake would not be persuaded to return to the car – were squashed into the little guard house, looking at the previous day's footage. And there he was, Marcus Featherstone, in his mother's red Panda, approaching the junction. Some sort of big BMW SUV came careening in the other direction, and nearly pushed him off the road. Marcus stopped his car. The SUV stopped too. Someone got out and took two steps towards Marcus's car. Angry steps, thought Julia. The driver had his back to her, but his body language was all pent up and angry, his coat swinging. He clearly thought better of it, stopped, waved his fist, and got back into the car. Julia had the disturbing sense that she'd just seen a violence narrowly averted. Both cars drove off, the big SUV going the way that Marcus had come from – and then there was Marcus, heading to Hayfield.

Julia contained her delight at her discovery, covering it with a sigh. 'You know, Ned, I realise, the angle's not right. We were just out of the shot, I won't be able to see anything. Thanks for trying, though, you've been very kind.'

He seemed crestfallen on her behalf. 'I'm so sorry. Should we try one of the other cameras?'

'I've taken enough of your time. You've been great. Thanks so much, Ned.'

'My pleasure, Mrs Bird. Nice to meet you and Jake. See you around, I'm sure.'

'No doubt,' she said, feeling a little guilty at her duplicity. 'And send our regards to your Jake.'

24

Hayfield was only six miles away, according to the signpost at the junction. Julia decided to make good her promise to Jake and take him to the castle. Not that Jake cared where they went, as long as they were out and about. But she'd never been to Hayfield herself, and she was always saying she should explore the surrounding area more.

While she drove down the country road, she admired the patches of sun and shade running across the landscape as the clouds moved overhead, and went through in her mind what she knew about Hayfield. It had the castle, of course. There was apparently a very good gastro pub, it was on all the lists, the Something & Something. She forgot the name. They were all the Something & Something. Pig & Whistle, Slug & Lettuce, Rose & Ha'penny.

Someone had mentioned the village recently; she tried to remember when. It came to her in a flash – Marcus! When she'd met him at the Garden Centre, he'd mentioned his fiancée lived there. What had he said?

'Milly, she's a local girl. She's a yoga teacher at the studio over in Hayfield.' Julia felt herself blush, even though she was all alone, at the thought that she hadn't remembered this before. Hadn't Hayley been complaining to Walter that she didn't know where the girlfriend lived, and all along, Julia had known. She just hadn't remembered.

A sign indicated Hayfield Castle to her left, the village of Hayfield straight ahead. Julia's foot hovered over the brake, her hand on the indicator.

'Sorry, Jake,' she said, shifting her foot and pressing down on the accelerator. 'We'll do a long walk tomorrow to make up for it. Promise.'

The centre of the village of Hayfield was similar to Berrywick, with its stone row houses and cobbled lanes, but it was even smaller, with just one main shopping road. Julia parked her car and typed 'yoga Hayfield' into Google. There were two yoga establishments listed. One belonged to someone called Tim, and seemed to be in Tim's bedsit, with his sleeping cat and the edge of his washing machine visible in the photograph. The other was a small studio with pale wooden floors and white walls. It was at the far end of the main road, past the shops. Julia decided to try that one.

The class seemed to have just finished. The glass door opened and out came three women in stretchy leggings with rolled-up mats under their arms and the glow of health and tranquillity on their faces – or perhaps Julia imagined that last part.

'Thanks, Milly!' said the last one over her shoulder as she left. 'Great class.'

'My pleasure, Siobhan. Have a peaceful evening.'

Julia grabbed the door as Siobhan released it, and stepped into the small studio. A woman was stacking foam blocks neatly onto a shelf, her back to the door.

'Milly?' asked Julia.

The young woman dropped a block in surprise and turned sharply. 'Oh, I didn't hear you come in. Hello.' She took a breath and gave Julia a welcoming smile. Her shiny black hair was tied in a low ponytail, loosely held back from a round, gentle face.

'I'm sorry, Milly, I didn't mean to startle you,' Julia said, picking up the block and handing it back to her. 'I'm looking for Marcus. I haven't been able to get him on the phone and I thought you might be able to help me.'

'Oh.' A tiny frown crossed Milly's smooth brow. 'He's not on his phone. He is here at my flat, but he's resting. Perhaps you could give him a call next week. He hasn't been very well the last day or so. He's taking a digital detox. No phone, no computers. Total calm and relaxation.' She paused and smiled. 'It was my idea, and I think it's helping him.'

'I know it's been a hard time for him, with everything that's happened with St Martin's.' Julia kept her comment deliberately vague. She had no idea how much Milly knew. Or how much Marcus knew, for that matter. Or how suspicious Milly would be of a strange woman who had arrived unannounced and started asking questions.

'That's it exactly,' said Milly, who seemed to be a very trusting soul. She looked relieved to have someone understanding to talk to. 'All those memories. It's been very unsettling for him.'

'And the headteacher...' Julia left this sentence open. Did Milly know that the headteacher was dead? Murdered, perhaps by Marcus.

'Yes, he went to see Mr Schofield yesterday. I think it was the right thing to do. Get things out in the open. Clear the air so that Marcus can move on.'

It was clear that Milly didn't know about Mr Schofield's death.

Julia took a breath. 'Yes, well, we need to talk about Mr Schofield.'

Marcus, already naturally pale-skinned, had turned ashen. His freckles were stark against the grey-white of his cheeks.

'What?' he said, with a slow blink of his blue eyes. 'What do you mean, dead?'

'Mr Schofield died yesterday,' said Julia, in the calm, patient way she had repeated bad news many times in her life.

Marcus shook his head as if that would shake something loose, something to make this news make sense. 'That can't... I mean... I just saw him. Yesterday morning.'

He frowned and opened his mouth and closed it, like a fish. It was clear that he was struggling to comprehend this fact – that the man had previously been alive, and was now, apparently, dead.

'Come and sit down, my love,' said Milly, taking his hand gently in hers and leading him to the two-seater sofa that took up most of the wall of the tiny bedsit, which was behind the larger room that was the studio, connected by a sliding door.

The young couple sat down. Julia took one of the other two chairs in the place, a wooden kitchen chair at a small counter. Milly and Marcus were both small-boned and delicate in build, but even so, with the addition of Julia, the room was crowded.

'Your mum and dad told me you went to visit Mr Schofield, to talk to him about your time at St Martin's, and how he let you down.'

'You spoke to Mum and Dad?' Marcus said.

'Yes,' she said, without explanation. She moved quickly into her questions: 'Can you tell me about your meeting, Marcus?'

'I needed to get things off my chest, after all that business with Mrs Benjamin. I realised that *he* was the one at fault. *He* should have done something. I spoke to Milly' – the girl nodded and smiled serenely – 'and she said I couldn't carry around all this pain and anger. I must let it out, get rid of it.'

'Anger is poisonous,' said Milly. 'To the body and the soul.' She did a vague hand movement that seemed to imply that your body lived in your stomach, and your soul in your chest.

'I decided I would tell him my feelings, and then move on. The next morning, I woke up feeling better. It felt so good to be taking action, finally. I didn't wait. I got out of bed and drove straight to his house.'

'You knew where he lived?'

'Looked it up,' he said, in answer to her silly question. 'I got there early, about eight. Knocked on the door. He was surprised to see me, of course, but he let me in. I told him straight off that I needed to tell him exactly what had happened to me, and his part in it. I was shaking, I tell you. It wasn't easy. But he invited me into his study, made me a cup of cocoa, and listened. For the first time, someone at the school listened.'

Marcus's voice caught in his throat and his eyes misted over. Milly leaned into him, her head on his shoulder.

'How did he respond?' asked Julia.

'Better than I could imagine. He listened without a word, and then he apologised. He said that he'd failed in his duty to me. That he hadn't done enough to protect certain children from Mrs Benjamin. That he'd been taken in by her, and he had been too focused on the results she was getting. He said that there had been something else, and he shouldn't have let it matter, but he did, and he was wrong. I didn't really know what he meant by that, but he took full responsibility and made a heartfelt apology. That's what mattered to me.'

Julia was surprised. 'I must say, that's quite something. Acknowledgement of fault and true apology are rare, in my experience.'

'When you say your experience... I'm sorry, but... who are

you? I mean... If I remember, you said you were a psychologist or something?'

'I'm a social worker.'

'Do you work for the school?'

'No. Not officially. I'm retired.'

'Oh yes, you said.'

Milly and Marcus looked at Julia expectantly, waiting for her to explain what exactly she was doing there in their little bedsit, questioning Marcus. She decided to come clean. 'I have no official role here. I found Ursula Benjamin's body. I've assisted unofficially with the police. I hate bullying with a great passion. And I can't abide a mystery in need of solving. I'm a bit of a busybody, if I must be honest.'

Marcus nodded as if this made perfect sense, which of course it didn't at all. Julia had no right to be here and was on very shaky ground. She felt a rush of unease at the thought of Hayley's reaction when she heard that Julia had been poking about. She would not be pleased.

Marcus continued, 'Well, that's all I have to tell you. We talked for about half an hour, I suppose. He was a good guy. Good listener. I felt heard. I had closure.' He spoke the words with a slight awkwardness, and Julia suspected that Milly had given him the language to voice his experience.

'And then?'

'And then he told me he was sorry to rush me out, but he had a meeting shortly. A parent from the school, I think. Must have been important if they were coming to his house. Quite amazing though, he thanked me for coming. He said he was glad we'd had this chat. He'd done a lot of reflecting over the last week or so, he said. Reflection, maybe, he said. Something like that. Anyway, he said Mrs Benjamin's death and all the questions, you know, it had stirred up a lot of feelings for him too. Guilt, mostly, he said. Shame. He felt better too, having spoken about it. Same as me. Said I should come by at any time if I wanted to talk about things again.'

'And?'

'And I left.'

Julia hesitated and said, 'And when you left him, was he alive?'

'Alive? Of course he was alive. What do you... What are you asking? Oh my God, you don't think...?'

'Marcus, David Schofield didn't just die, he was murdered. You are going to have to talk to the police. They know you were there right before he was killed.'

25

DC Walter Farmer had phoned Julia back just as she finished talking to Marcus and Milly, and rejoined the dejected Jake. She sat in her parked car and filled Walter in on her discoveries. Well, some of them. She left out the duplicitousness around the CCTV cameras – it was a grave overstep, and besides, she still felt rather bad about poor Ned, who was no doubt wondering which exact house in Fairweather Estate she lived in with his dog's namesake. Instead, she skipped straight to the part where she'd remembered about Marcus's girlfriend living in Hayfield.

'I thought, perhaps it's all a misunderstanding, and he was with her, rather than on the run somewhere. I was in the village anyway, with Jake. We were going to go for a walk at the castle.'

'I hear it's very nice,' Walter said. 'I've been meaning to go.'

Julia didn't offer an opinion on the castle, not wanting to draw attention to the fact that she hadn't actually visited, on account of being too busy snooping in police business.

'Anyway, I thought I'd pop by Milly's work and just ask her if he was with her and if he was okay. Checking up, as a concerned acquaintance, you know. I tried to get hold of you when I thought of it. That was the first thing I did,' she said, somewhat truthfully.

'Yes, I know you did. I called as soon as I saw your message.' Walter was a very understanding fellow; Julia was fairly sure his superior would be significantly less so.

'Well, I couldn't get hold of you, but I did see a yoga studio, right there on the main road. You can't miss it. So I went in and had a word. I had no intention of speaking to Marcus at all, just to find out where he was, but as it turned out he was there. He was in her flat, attached to the yoga studio. When I told her about Mr Schofield, Milly went and called him. There was really nothing I could do but listen.'

'You'd better come in right now,' said Walter with a deep sigh. 'The boss needs to hear this. And she's not going to like it.'

He was right about that.

At the station, DC Farmer ushered Julia into a meeting room and went to call DI Hayley Gibson, who had already been briefed.

'I'll leave you to it,' said Walter. He clearly could not wait to get away, knowing full well that things were about to get ugly between his boss and the interfering Julia Bird. 'I'm going to go and fetch Marcus and bring him in for an interview. Goodbye, Mrs Bird.' There was a ring of sad finality to Walter's 'goodbye', as if he suspected he might never see her again.

It seemed like the mere sound of Walter saying 'Mrs Bird' made Hayley wince. She was furious with Julia. Furious. As Julia had known she would be.

Julia had been able to see no way of imparting the information she had got from Marcus without a full confession, so came right out with it. By the second sentence, waves of conflicting emotion were crossing Hayley's face like the dappled shade and sun Julia had seen on the hill. Except there was no sun. Only a mix of disbelief, anger, confusion – and, yes, interest.

'You spoke to the suspect. You compromised a police investigation,' the detective said angrily. 'I've half a mind to charge you with obstruction.'

'Hayley, I'm sorry, I…'

'Cut it. Finish the story.'

Julia told her story, just as she'd told Walter – Milly, the yoga studio, the surprise appearance of Marcus – and his meeting with the head. Hayley listened, stony-faced. There was a slight warming up when she heard about the meeting the head had apparently arranged for the morning of the murder.

'With a parent, you say?'

'That's what Marcus said that he said.'

'Did he say anything else? Name? Time? What it was about?'

Julia shook her head.

Hayley picked up her phone without explanation, dialled and said, 'Walter, where are you? Okay good, you're almost there. Listen, don't get Marcus. Go straight to Schofield's house, you're round the corner. See if you can find a diary. A note. Anything to tell us who he was meeting that morning or why. Phone me when you get there. In the meantime, I'll try and get access to his phone records. There might be a message, or something in his electronic calendar.'

Hayley picked up the phone in the meeting room and dialled a few short digits, an internal call presumably, to an underling, who she instructed to apply for access to Schofield's phone. The phone clattered into its cradle.

There was a heavy silence between the two women. Julia broke it with what she hoped was a helpful piece of information. 'One thing I noticed about Marcus is that he's a small guy with small feet. No way he wears a size ten shoe. He's a six or a seven, I'd say. Just a bit bigger than mine, and I'm a five. He wouldn't be a match for the prints you found at the two crime scenes.'

'We'll let forensics decide that one, shall we?' said Hayley, in a tone so clipped it could have trimmed a hedge into the shape of a peacock, something Julia had seen with her own eyes at one of the stately homes nearby.

'Of course,' Julia said meekly. 'I just...'

'Well, I'd better get back to the case,' the DI said, gathering her notebook and phone, in preparation for her exit.

Julia went for a last *mea culpa*. 'Hayley, I'm sorry. I did get a little carried away, once Marcus was actually in the room. I shouldn't have spoken to him. I should have left it and called you.'

'Yes. That's exactly what you should have done.'

'Right. I won't make this mistake again.'

Hayley gave a most unamused laugh, which emerged as a bitter, barking *gha* sound, and said, 'I very much doubt that's true. You are incorrigible.'

Julia took heart from the tiniest hint of affection in that last statement, and hoped that she and the DI would repair their friendship.

The two women stood up to go. DI Gibson's phone rang.

'What have you found?'

Infuriatingly, Walter's voice was indistinct to Julia. She stood motionless, watching Hayley's face. It relaxed a little; there was a shine in her eyes.

'A name?'

More indistinct muttering from Walter Farmer.

'Smith? That's it? Dear God in heaven, the most common surname in the whole of the British Isles?'

Julia waited while Walter spoke, presumably in the affirmative.

'Mr? Mrs? Doctor? Professor? Anything? Or a time?'

Walter spoke some more.

'Well okay, Walter, thanks. If you find anything else, phone me immediately.'

Hayley sat down again. Julia hovered a moment and followed her example. 'That's a bit rough. Smith.'

'Yup. Scrawled on the page. No time. No initial. Could be a reminder to phone the rat catcher, for all I know. Or a meeting with Mr Schofield's podiatrist.'

'Although, it's likely to be the parent that he was meeting, isn't it? Given what Marcus said. If it's the only word on that day's page.' Julia spoke tentatively, not wanting to annoy Hayley further with her assumptions.

'Yes, but we won't know until we've done the police work – made a list of names, got in contact, checked their alibis. Possible motives. Police work.' She emphasised the last two words pointedly, and added for good measure: 'Police work, as opposed to running about speculating and speaking to possible suspects.'

Julia knew she'd have to put up with a few more of these sorts of comments before Hayley let the matter rest.

'It could be a good lead, though, assuming it's not the podiatrist or the rat catcher,' she said brightly. 'I mean, once you find this Smith, if there's a connection to the school, there's a good chance you've got your man for the headteacher's murder.'

Hayley forgot for a moment that she'd cut Julia off, and mused out loud. 'Yes, and likely Mrs Benjamin's murder, too. My working hypothesis is that the killers of Mrs Benjamin and Mr Schofield are one and the same. There's the footprint match. And of course the fact that the two victims work together. Whoever it is, he's most likely connected to the school.'

Julia phrased her own thoughts as a tentative question, given the shaky ground on which she walked: 'So, do you think it's a parent, or perhaps an adult pupil? One of the boys Ursula bullied, grown up and angry? Perhaps a teacher, or some other staff member?'

'Yes. Although we don't know the motive, there might be a link we haven't uncovered yet. But first things first. I'll get in touch with the school and see if I can get a list. I'll probably need another bloody warrant. But I'll find me a Smith, whatever it takes.'

'Can't be too many Smiths in one school, can there?'

'We'll soon find out, won't we?'

Julia felt a little encouraged by the word 'we'. Perhaps she wasn't going to be out in the cold forever.

'Well, I'll let you get on with it. Don't want to keep you from your work. Good luck, Hayley, and once again I really am sorry.'

Hayley looked no friendlier, but she waved Julia's apology away. 'Okay, okay. Off you go. I've got work to do now that Marcus Featherstone's small feet make him a less likely suspect. Starting with that list.' She didn't mention that it was thanks to Julia that the small feet were on the table, so to speak, but Julia liked to imagine that there was some acknowledgment of a job well done in her tone.

Julia arrived home feeling rather buoyant. She realised that this was the buoyancy akin to that of a convict on Death Row who'd been given a last-minute reprieve. Somewhat less dramatically, she had survived the fury of DI Gibson. It was over and done with.

Julia woke late the next morning. Once the chickens and Jake had had their breakfast, Julia was looking forward to a couple of her hens' fresh eggs, scrambled, on hot buttered toast. Jake, of course, was looking forward to a walk.

'Breakfast first,' Julia said, taking a bowl and a plate from the shelf. 'Then walk.'

Recognising the word, Jake ran for the door, his tail wagging eagerly. He let out three short barks.

'Quiet, Jake. Not yet. In a minute. I said breakfast... Oh, never mind.' She put a slice of sourdough bread into the toaster. 'But come on, let's pick some chives and a bit of thyme.'

Jake bolted into the garden. He certainly was an eager chap; it was one of the things she liked about him. You never got a 'no thanks, I'll sit this one out' from Jake. As for Julia, she still got a thrill from harvesting her own produce, whether it was the day's lay, or a plum from the tree, or a handful of leaves for a salad.

Herbs at the ready, Julia cracked the first brown-shelled egg against the counter and emptied the contents into the bowl. She did the same with the second. Only when she'd had her own laying hens had she realised what a poor imitation the supermarket eggs were. Her eggs were big, the large yolks more orange than yellow, the white thick and firm. Scrambled in plenty of butter and topped with a few snipped herbs from the garden, they were heaven on a plate. She took a fork to them and planned her day.

'A quick walk by the water, and I'll drop you home,' she told Jake, pouring the eggs into the bubbling pan. 'I'll go back to town to do the shopping. Sean's coming for supper, and we need a few things. I thought I'd do lamb chops.' Jake looked as if he approved of her choice. 'And after that I'll need some time on the computer. I've got a bit of admin to take care of.' Jake had no idea what she was talking about, obviously, but he looked at her with love and admiration, as if he thought every word a gem.

They went straight out after breakfast, following the familiar route down to the river. The regulars were out, of course. Yorkie lady. Runner with border collies. Auntie Edna on her regular circuit.

Julia thought about Edna. She knew so little about her. Everyone else in the village had known the woman forever, and just accepted her strange presence. She was apparently well-cared for, and the general feeling was that she was safe enough, walking the familiar paths around the river.

'Good morning, Edna,' Julia said.

'Good morning to you,' Edna replied, politely uttering the correct response to a question for a change. Except that she addressed Jake. 'Are you well?'

Julia hesitated, then said on his behalf, 'Yes, thank you. Very well.'

Edna patted Jake's head and said, 'Pleased to hear it. Expect the rain, rain again. And again from Spain. Pitter patter.'

'Thank you, we'll take an umbrella,' said Julia.

Edna straightened up and looked at her as if she were an idiot. 'What for?'

Julia was stumped for an answer. She noted, as Edna walked off, that she was no longer wearing Ursula Benjamin's striped scarf. Presumably the police had taken it as evidence. She hadn't thought to ask, not that Hayley was taking questions from Julia at this point. Had they questioned Edna about how and where she'd got the scarf? She couldn't imagine they'd gotten anything sensible from her.

It struck Julia that, assuming she was right, and Edna had found the scarf in one of the Berrywick dustbins, there was a reasonably limited number of dustbins from which she might have taken it. Julia crossed paths with her down by the river most days. As far as she could tell, the old woman didn't range far and wide. It seemed Edna took the same route every day.

Julia looked at the old woman's retreating back for a long minute. She turned and gave a little tug of Jake's lead, 'Change of plan, Jake. We're going this way.' And she set off after Edna.

26

Up the river path heading away from the village centre, across the little park, down Stonehill Way, and back again past the sweet shop. Julia followed Edna all the way, and into the tiny shop – more of a kiosk, really – with its red and white sign saying simply *Sweeties*.

Not being much of a sweet eater herself, Julia seldom went in, but when she did, she appreciated the sheer comprehensiveness of the offering. It was a treasure trove for sweet lovers, with thousands of sweets. It stocked all the old favourites that Julia remembered from her childhood – mint humbugs, sherbet lemons, pear drops, acid drops, jelly babies and dolly mixtures, some of them in great big jars.

The woman behind the counter was nearly as old as Edna, but the exact opposite in stature – short and round, against Edna's more elongated, albeit stooped, bony frame. Her cheerful pink-cheeked face, framed by a mass of soft white curls, only just cleared the top of the row of jars. If one of those chubby cherubs in a Renaissance painting grew up, that's what it would look like, thought Julia.

The woman waited without the least impatience while

Edna surveyed the merchandise, starting at one end of the counter, and tottering slowly along to the other side. She repeated the exercise in the other direction, paying full attention to each offering, and turned to face the shopkeeper, who asked with a smile. 'What'll it be this morning, Edna?'

'Liquorice Allsorts please, Dora. Small packet.'

'Ah, good choice,' said Dora, reaching for them.

'Oh, and it's you!' Edna said, when she spotted Julia and Jake behind her. 'Bye bad boy, give the big bad boy a bone.'

Dora handed over the sweets – 'There, you go, dear' – and accepted a coin from Edna. Julia noted that it was a five pence coin, which she was fairly sure wasn't the going rate for Liquorice Allsorts. Even the small packet.

'You take care now on your way home. Enjoy your sweets. See you tomorrow.'

'Allsort and anysort. My regards to Fred. Good evening, Dora.'

'And the same to you.'

Edna left, the shopkeeper looking after her. There was sadness on her cherubic face, and she muttered, 'Except that it's not yet noon, and our Fred gone seven years in July.'

She addressed Julia in a louder voice, 'And what can I get for you?'

Despite her preference for the savoury over sweet, Julia was moved by nostalgia to buy a selection of the old-fashioned sweets she'd enjoyed as a child. 'Humbugs, please. Ooh, you have rhubarb and custard, I'd completely forgotten about those. I used to love them,' she said. Luckily, she always brought a few pounds in her pocket, just in case. 'I'll take a few of each, please.'

Dora smiled at Julia's eagerness, and filled up a packet with her requests.

'That'll be two pounds twenty. Are you visiting the area?' Dora asked, chattily.

'I live here, but I'm fairly new. I know Edna from my walks.'

'Regular as clockwork she is, round and round she goes.'

'Where does she live?'

'At the end of the lane. She does her walk, two or three times a day, and stops here on her way home for a little treat. She's all right is Edna, we all keep an eye on her. Better than being shut up somewhere, isn't it?'

'It certainly is,' Julia said, thinking of the lonely lives some old people lived in the city. 'She's lucky to live in a safe place where people know her.'

A little girl came in. She couldn't have been more than six, but there was no sign of a parent. 'Hello, Miss Dora. Can I have jelly babies for this, please?' She opened her tightly closed hand to reveal a pound coin.

'Of course, Lulu.' Dora reached for the jellies and handed them over. The little girl left, already digging into the packet of sweets before she was out the door.

Julia followed her lead and popped a rhubarb and custard into her mouth. Memories of childhood holidays on a windswept Welsh beach flooded back to her.

'Delicious, just as good as I remember,' Julia said. 'Thank you, Dora. Nice to meet you. I'm Julia, by the way. Julia Bird.'

'Ah yes, I've heard of *you*,' said Dora. 'Welcome to Berrywick. And don't eat those all at once!'

Julia set off for home, running through Edna's route in her mind. She wished she'd brought a paper and pen to make a note of the roads and houses, and more importantly, the dustbins. But she never took anything on her walks. Except Jake, of course, and a bit of cash. A few houses down from the sweet shop, she turned and went back.

'Goodness. Finished them already?' Dora asked in mock surprise.

Julia chuckled. 'No. I wondered, do you sell pens and paper? I need to make a note.'

'I don't sell them, but I can give you a pen and paper. A page of this do?' she asked, pointing to an A4 exercise book on the counter.

'That would be perfect!'

Dora tore a page off and handed it over. 'And I'm sure to have a pencil to spare.'

She opened a drawer beneath the counter and, after a bit of scrabbling, found a short pencil with a ring of teeth marks at the end of it. She held it up, and raised her eyebrows. 'This all right?'

'Perfect,' said Julia again, reaching into her pocket for her money. 'Let me...'

Dora waved her money away.

'Thanks, Dora.'

'You're most welcome, Julia Bird.'

Julia retraced the loop that Edna had walked, and made a simple map, noting the names of the roads, as well as the placement of the houses, the river, and a few other distinguishing features. She came full circle, passing her own home, before arriving at the last house before the little wooded area and the lane that led to the sweet shop and Edna's house. When she'd finished, she stopped and leaned against a low wall, took out her sweets and popped a celebratory humbug into her mouth. She looked at her piece of paper with satisfaction and sucked on the sweet. What did the map tell her? Well, there were only twenty-eight houses on her route, one length being entirely taken up by river. So that was something. But not much, she thought, somewhat deflated.

Jake tugged at his lead, interrupting her reverie. 'Okay, we're going,' she said, looking up from the paper. To her horror, coming towards her was DI Hayley Gibson. How would she explain that she was once again investigating something? Jake must have spotted Hayley getting out of her car, which was parked further up the road. He was tugging at his lead in eager recognition.

'Hello. What are you doing here?' Julia asked Hayley, hoping to distract Hayley from asking her that question. It was not to be.

'I could ask you the same,' said the detective, fending off Jake's enthusiastic welcome, which involved turning in a figure-of-eight and bashing into both women's legs as he did so. The movement was accompanied by some high-pitched whining.

'Our daily walk. We're always out and about, aren't we, Jake? Would you like a rhubarb and custard?' She held out the bag to Hayley.

'A what?'

'A sweetie. I've also got humbugs. I bought them from the little sweet shop. It is like the 1970s in there.'

Hayley looked blank, but took one and put it in her mouth.

'How did your Smith hunt go?' Julia asked.

'Zizzweet iz good. Went awigtht,' Hayley mumbled through a mouthful of sweet. 'Hound a hew Shmishs.'

'You found a few Smiths? Oh well, that's good,' Julia said, slipping her map into her pocket.

'Wha's hat?'

'What?'

'That paper?'

'Oh, this. Well, you won't need it now, if your Smith search pans out. But it's a record of Edna's route. She does the same route every day. So it's a map of where she goes, and the houses she passes.'

'You followed her?'

'Well, we were going in the same direction. And I thought... In case you wanted to follow up on the scarf, at any point. Because she would have got it from the dustbin of one of the houses on this route, most likely.'

Hayley had reduced the sweet to manageable proportions and spoke more clearly. 'DC Farmer has been looking into the scarf. He spoke to Edna, but he couldn't get anything useful out of her.'

'No, I would have thought not.'

'The scarf has been sent for testing, but it's been in a dustbin and all about the village on Edna's neck for days, so I'm not optimistic that it'll be helpful in terms of the killer's DNA. Or in fact, anything.'

'It doesn't sound likely. But if you have found your Smith, that's the main thing.' Julia was dying to hear more about Smith, but didn't want to push her luck with a direct enquiry.

'I wouldn't say I've found my Smith. There is only one Smith family in the school. I phoned Mr Bernard Smith, father of James Smith, in Year Eight. His wife Marion answered, and said that he was in South America on business. Flew from London Heathrow the day before Ursula died, and he'll be home on Sunday. My people checked with the airlines and confirmed that this was indeed the case. Which means that Bernard Smith did not kill Ursula Benjamin, nor was he scheduled to meet David Schofield on the day of his murder, and nor did he kill Schofield. On account of being thousands of miles away at the time.'

The words rushed out of her and when she'd finished, she took a deep breath and let out a deep sigh of frustration.

'Oh, I am sorry. It seemed like such a good lead. So it's back to square one.'

'Not quite. There's one other Smith-ish family, the Pottington-Smiths. It might be them. But it seems like a long shot.'

'It's worth a try, I suppose.'

'Yes. Could I see your map?'

Julia pulled the crumpled paper from her pocket, laid it on

top of the wall and smoothed it out with the flat of her hand. 'It's a little rough, but this is the basic route Edna follows every day. She lives in this lane, here...' she pointed. 'And she walks past the sweet shop... here... and she travels a loop, like this.' She traced the black line with her finger, giving the paper a couple of sharp taps. 'Now, as you can see, much of the walk is along the river, and there are no houses and hence no dustbins there. And on the other side, you've got the park. I counted, and all in all there are only twenty-eight houses on her route. It seems to me that it wouldn't be too difficult to go door to door and check them out. If one was so inclined.'

Hayley ran her fingers through her short hair in an upward movement, creating a crown of dark spikes. Her frustration had dissipated; her blue eyes were bright and eager. 'Yes indeed, although we might not need to go door to door.' She gave Julia a teasing smile. It was a nice change from the general air of irritation and stress that she'd been giving off, at least in Julia's presence.

'Why not?'

'Well, interestingly, Bernard and Marion Smith live here.' Hayley stabbed at the paper. 'Which would be exciting if we hadn't already ruled him out. But the Pottington-Smiths live right here.' Hayley stabbed a finger at the paper again. 'Twenty-Seven Bay Tree Lane.' Julia looked down, and then up at the street. Sure enough, there on the wall across the road from them was the road name: Bay Tree Lane. They both looked back at the paper and then up and to the right, down the row of houses. Hayley pointed.

'Over there, on the left. On Edna's rubbish route, if your theory and your map are correct.'

'Goodness, if that's right, that means...'

'It means it's time I made the acquaintance of Mr Pottington-Smith.'

27

Say what you like about Mr Pottington-Smith, his feet were plenty big enough. In unison, Julia and Hayley raised their eyes from his feet – easily a ten, if not an eleven, in Julia's estimation. In fact, the whole of Mr Pottington-Smith was big and solid, from his domed head, through the shelf of his shoulders, over the barrel of his chest, to his muscular thighs. And his feet.

'Can I help you?' he asked the two women, who were standing at his front gate. He had arrived from up the lane just moments after their own arrival from the other direction. He was accompanied by a bull terrier – huge, it must be said – on a thick chain with a studded leather collar. The two dogs eyed each other. One a soppy chocolate Lab, the other a hunk of solid muscle. Julia took a couple of steps back to create some space between them. Jake stayed with her and when she stopped, pressed himself against Julia's leg and sat very still and very quiet, while Hayley asked the questions.

'Mr Pottington-Smith? Derek Pottington-Smith?'

He folded his thick arms across his chest. 'Who's asking?'

'Detective Hayley Gibson. Nothing to be concerned about, just a routine enquiry.'

'About what?'

'Are you Mr Pottington-Smith?'

'Derek. Yes.'

'Do you know a Mr David Schofield?'

'The headteacher? Yes, I know him. Or did. He's dead, isn't he?'

'Correct. We're speaking to people in the community who knew him.'

'Can't say I *knew* him. He went to the same gym as me. Riverclub Fitness Centre. I teach the boxing class.' All the muscles in his upper body twitched in a ripple effect when he said this. It was a remarkable thing to witness, but Julia couldn't work out whether it was a deliberate display or something involuntary. 'He didn't come to my class. He was into spinning.' He moved his hands around briefly in a circular motion, as if they were feet on pedals. 'Some people like it, you know, on the bikes, not going anywhere. Spinning.' There was a slight curl to Derek Pottington-Smith's lip at the concept of spinning. He added, rather unnecessarily: 'We didn't talk much.'

'But you saw him around the place regularly?'

'Yeah.'

'I see,' said Hayley, keeping her tone level. 'When did you last see Mr Schofield?'

'Couldn't say. Probably Monday or Tuesday? I reckon I saw him there this week, at any rate. Before he, you know, passed. But why are you asking me about Schofield?'

'I understand you are a parent at the school. You have a child there?'

'Benny. Yeah.'

'Did Ursula Benjamin teach him?'

'Yeah.'

'Is your son happy at St Martin's?' Hayley asked.

Derek Pottington-Smith shrugged and frowned, as if to indicate that this was a question to which he couldn't possibly be expected to know the answer.

'Do you have many dealings with the school?'

'When I have to.'

'And the headteacher?'

'Likewise.'

Blood from a stone, thought Julia. Either he really had nothing to say on the subject of Mr Schofield, or he was being cagey.

A few fat drops of rain fell, with the promise of many more to follow from the thick grey cloud that brooded above their heads.

'If there's nothing else, I'll be getting inside,' Derek Pottington-Smith said. A statement, rather than a question. He stepped forward and made to manoeuvre his big frame between Hayley and the gate. The bull terrier eyed Hayley with what Julia and Jake took to be malevolence. They both took a further step back, to be well out of his way. Hayley hesitated and did the same, addressing Derek Pottington-Smith's broad back. 'I have a few more questions, if you don't mind. It won't take long. Could I come inside for a minute?'

'No,' came the reply.

'Did you have an appointment to see Mr Schofield earlier this week? Your name is in his appointment book,' she called after him. 'Where were you on Wednesday morning, Mr Pottington-Smith?'

Derek Pottington-Smith opened his front door and turned to face her. He gave her a long, steady look, and said, 'I can see this is all going to take a bit longer than I thought. Give me ten minutes. I just need to sort some things out here, and then I can come down to the station.'

. . .

'Look at us, going somewhere new,' said Tabitha, only half joking. They did rather gravitate towards the Buttered Scone, the library, or Julia's kitchen table.

'And for brunch, too,' Julia said from behind a large menu. Tabitha gave a snort of laughter. Brunch was a standing joke between the two of them since the earliest days of their acquaintance, when they'd first heard the term from the lips of Sophie Billington, a pretentious girl in their first-year English class. They had both burst out laughing in delight at the new word, and the ridiculousness of the notion of a meal that was both breakfast and lunch. Their friendship was set. That had been forty years ago.

'Have to say, it all sounds delicious. "Artisanal sourdough French toast with organic crème fraîche and hand-picked raspberries dusted with lavender sugar."'

'Gosh.' Tabitha picked up her own menu. 'That sounds like it would see you through to lupper.'

'Or linner.'

They laughed loudly at their own joke, startling a passing waitress who came over and offered to take their drinks orders. The coffee menu was so overwhelming that Julia ordered tea. Tabitha was more stalwart in the face of the beverage list, and ordered a macchiato.

'What's that one again?' Julia asked. 'Is that the one with cocoa in it?'

'Who knows?' Tabitha waved her arm nonchalantly, the wide sleeve of her kaftan making a beautiful sweep of red, gold and green stripes, like a ship's sail. She always looked quite stylish in a funky librarian sort of way, but she looked particularly fine this morning. Julia complimented her on the gorgeous dress.

'My cousin brought it over for me.'

'From Ghana?'

'Of course, from Ghana. You don't think any of Dad's Welsh relatives would come up with something like this? Amma's daughter, Angela, the youngest, is here looking at uni. She brought it. You don't think it's too much for Berrywick?'

'Oh, definitely too much. It's exactly what the place needs.' It was true that even on a Saturday morning in the Lemon Café, the hot new spot on the road between Berrywick and Edgely, no one could touch Tabitha's outfit for style. A fair number of the customers seemed to be straight from the gym, wearing workout gear and shiny ponytails. They were downing shot glasses of lurid fruit drinks laced with heaven-knew-what.

'Well, the life I lead, I'd wait until Christmas for a chance to wear my new dress, and by then it's so cold we're all wearing spencers and parkas and fur-lined boots. It's not as if I've got a fancy doctor *beau* like *some people*. How are things with Sean, speaking of?'

'He was round for supper last night. I don't know, Tabitha, I couldn't be more surprised to find myself in...' Julia paused, not sure whether the next word she was looking for was 'love' or 'a relationship'. 'We get on very well. We've got lots to talk about. He's a good man. A kind man. It almost seems too good to be true.'

'Not too good. Just good. As you deserve. Just enjoy it. You've got a chap who's crazy about you and is just perfect in so many ways. The dogs like each other. He makes a mean bolognaise. And if you cut your finger slicing onions, he can bandage it up for you.'

'Yes, there's that, and he's got the whole 007 thing going for him.' Julia made a poor imitation of a gun with her fingers, like the Bond logo, and blew imaginary smoke off the top.

'Ah yes, well. That'll do it. Licence to thrill and all.'

The waitress came back with their drinks just in time for another round of raucous laughter, accompanied, in Julia's case, by a hot blush across her cheeks.

'Glad to see you ladies are having fun,' the waitress said, with a touch of wistfulness. Who didn't love a good laugh with a friend? 'Now, let's see if we can make the day even better, shall we? What'll you be having to eat?'

Over artisanal sourdough French toast – it was everything it promised on the menu – and Tabitha's deconstructed eggs Benedict, they discussed the latest developments in the Ursula Benjamin murder investigation, which was now also the David Schofield murder investigation. As she was not officially involved with the case, and therefore not bound by any disclosure rules, Julia felt that she could spill the beans on the previous day's activities to her brunch companion. She held Tabitha enthralled with her description of the big taciturn boxing fellow and his muscle dog.

Tabitha leaned in and asked in a whisper, 'So do you think he killed them?'

'I don't know. He knows the head from the school and from the Riverclub Fitness Centre. He's got a kid at the school and in Ursula Benjamin's class. He's on Edna's walking route. There's the Smith name in the book. He's got big enough feet. That's quite a few bits of the puzzle fitting together, but it all seems quite circumstantial to me. I only met him briefly, but it doesn't feel right.'

'What about him makes you think he's not the guy?'

'The main thing is, he just didn't seem that concerned about his son. The way I see it, the motive for these murders has to be related to the school, and to Ursula's behaviour. Whoever killed these two people was angry or vengeful because of the way their child was treated. When Hayley asked Smith whether his son was happy at the school, he didn't seem to know. In fact, he didn't seem to really see the point of the question! He certainly didn't appear an engaged enough dad to start killing people at the school to protect his son's emotional health. I think about some of the parents at Jess's school, and let me tell you... There were some lovely people – Peter and I made good friends there – but when it came to their children, some of them seemed to lose all reason.'

There were a couple of mums whose level of engagement and protectiveness had been dangerously off the charts. One had relentlessly complained about a young teacher whom she believed – without a shred of evidence – undermined her child's confidence by correcting his spelling. She'd mobilised the other parents against her until the poor woman had left the school. Julia wouldn't be surprised if she'd left the entire profession. There had once been a lawsuit over a boy's place in a cricket tour – he hadn't been picked, and his parents thought he should have been. She could think of at least three more examples of outright madness.

'At a push, I could imagine one of those mothers going bonkers enough to get physical if she thought her child was in danger of being bullied. There is no reason to assume that the parents at St Martin's are any different. It's just that Derek Pottington-Smith didn't seem like the man to do it. And then...'

Julia hesitated a moment before moving onto the new information she'd received from Hayley later that evening, once she'd questioned Derek. Tabitha was the furthest thing from a gossip, and a simple, 'Just between us, okay?' was all Julia needed to say to be sure that anything she said would indeed stay between the two old friends. She continued, 'When Hayley questioned him, he was quite unforthcoming. Taciturn and grumpy. I thought he was going to shut her down. He didn't let her in when it started raining, but he agreed to come down to the station and answer her questions as soon as he'd fed the dog and sorted out supper for the kid. According to Hayley, he did exactly that, he came down to the station yesterday evening.'

'And what did he say?'

Julia took a bite of her French toast – no sense in letting it get cold – and chewed and swallowed it before answering. 'He was quite co-operative, apparently. It seems he's just not a very chatty chap, but he answered all her questions. He denied having an appointment with David Schofield, or visiting him. Or having anything to do with his death, of course. He said he was at the fitness centre where he works when Schofield was killed on Wednesday morning. Said he was teaching a boxing class. DC Farmer has already sent a request to the head office of the gym chain to get access to the information about who entered when. It's all swipe cards and computers now, of course. It's always tricky on the weekends to find someone to authorise that sort of thing, but I suppose they'll know next week whether he's telling the truth about his whereabouts. Or whether he killed the head.'

'It sounds as if it wasn't him, but even so, someone did it.' Tabitha put her coffee cup down hard. 'I don't know what the world's coming to, really I don't. People bullying children. Killing teachers. Strangling a woman with her own scarf!' Her voice rose at that last horror and drew shocked looks from two women with sleek matching blonde bobs who were drinking tiny coffees at the next table.

Julia kept her voice low, and put her hand over her friend's. 'It's awful to witness the violence and pain that goes on in the world, to have it so close. Let's hope Hayley will get her man and the law will take its course.'

Their buoyant mood had dimmed with all this talk of the basest human behaviour. They finished their meal in silence, and Julia had an idea. 'I know. Let's take a walk around the little centre. I've never seen this bit of the area and it will help me digest the organic sourdough raspberries.'

'That's a good idea, I don't come out this way much and when I do, I don't usually stop and explore.'

. . .

The Lemon Café was on the outside terrace of a small shopping precinct. The little cluster of shops were stocked with very pretty pricey things that neither Tabitha or Julia wanted or needed. Decor items, wildly expensive designer umbrellas, and so on. They played a game that they used to play as youngsters, imagining that they were allowed to pick one thing, and then painstakingly making their choices.

Julia found hers in a tiny shop devoted only to coffee-related things, its window full of jugs and plungers and gleaming espresso pots, and special spoons and milk-frothers. Julia briefly coveted a set of tiny red espresso cups on tiny red saucers just for their sheer Italian stylishness, although she knew she'd never use them. Tabitha fancied a peacock blue silk nightie and matching silk gown in the same blue, with red poppies sprinkled across the shoulders. 'Although Lord knows who I'd be wearing that for.' She said it with a laugh, but the joke had a touch of wistfulness in it.

'For yourself,' said Julia, and gave her a squeeze across the shoulders.

A full circuit completed, they exited onto the road behind the little centre. Across the road, right ahead of them, a red neon sign announced *Riverclub Fitness Centre*.

'Well that explains the preponderance of Lycra in the café,' Tabitha said. 'Quite a coincidence, isn't it?'

'That we were just talking about the Riverclub Fitness Centre, and here it is? Yes indeed. Although I suppose it's close to Derek's house and to Schofield's, and not far from the school. It makes sense.'

The two women stood a moment, staring at the sign, and the people coming in and out through the big glass doors, dressed in gym gear and carrying kitbags.

'You know, Tabitha, I've been thinking of getting into a new hobby. I'd be keen on getting fitter and stronger. I think it's time we found out about gym membership, don't you? See what it's all about?'

'Honestly, Julia Bird. There really is no stopping you.'

28

'So that's monthly then, is it?' Julia asked.

'Yes, that's right,' said the girl behind the desk in the tiny cubicle, who was Ling, Membership Consultant, according to her name tag. 'Your first month's free, and then it's a monthly charge. There's a discount for, um...' She looked from Julia to Tabitha nervously and, having decided they were indeed over sixty, plunged in with, 'Seniors.' She then appeared to lose her nerve. She blushed a fiery red, and stammered. 'I mean, if... or when...'

'Thank you, Ling, that's good to know,' said Tabitha, putting the young woman out of her misery. 'We would appreciate the discount if we do decide to sign up.'

The red cleared from Ling's cheeks and she gave Tabitha a grateful smile, revealing a mouth full of silver metal braces behind her glossy purple lips.

'We're interested in the classes, mostly,' Julia said. 'Can you tell us about those?'

The girl pulled a sheet of paper from the drawer and handed it to her. 'This is our timetable. As you can see, there's a lot of choice. Cardio, general fitness, strength, flexibility, yoga, Pilates, boxercise. At least six classes a day, seven days a week, so you'll always find something to suit your schedule and your own personal fitness goals.'

Julia briefly tried on the thought of having her own personal fitness goals. She imagined coming to the gym every day for classes, the workout gear, the pressed juice at the café afterwards, bathed in the righteous glow of the recently exercised. But then she remembered Jake, and knew that her fitness destiny lay on the lanes and paths of Berrywick and surrounds, and not in the yoga studio. And she remembered that she wasn't really signing up for the gym: she was there under false pretences, snooping for information.

Tabitha hadn't forgotten. 'Boxercise? That sounds interesting, what is it?' she asked. Julia glanced over, and saw that her friend seemed to be enjoying her part in this investigation. She was doing an excellent impression of someone eagerly awaiting information. Julia remembered that she had, after all, been in the am-dram troupe at uni.

'It's a boxing class. It's an amazing workout. The instructor, that's Derek Smith, he gets you moving, that's for sure. Upper and lower body. Cardio. Strength. The whole package. If you're keen on upping your fitness game, it's a great way to go. We've got all the equipment – gloves, pads, even boxing bags – so you don't need to buy anything special. It's Mondays, Wednesdays and Fridays.'

So it looked as if Derek's alibi was checking out, Julia thought. He would have been here last Wednesday morning, teaching boxercise. She wasn't wildly surprised. She'd never bought him as a perpetrator, somehow. There wasn't a strong enough motive, unless Hayley had uncovered something new and explosive about his relationship with the school.

'Thanks very much for your time, Ling,' she said, getting to her feet. 'You've been very helpful. We'll have a think about it and be in touch if we decide to join.'

Julia ran her eyes down the days and across the time slots. There it was.

Boxercise with Derek S. Wednesday.

But at five o'clock in the afternoon, not the morning as he'd claimed. And it appeared that in his everyday life, Derek dropped the double-barrelled name and went by Smith. Which was what had been written in David Schofield's diary.

'That was fun. I felt like the clever detective's trusty sidekick in a movie,' said Tabitha, putting her arm through her friend's as they walked back to the car. Julia couldn't help but smile at the spring in Tabitha's step and the way her eyes twinkled with mischievous delight. 'A feel-good story of two sixty-something ladies who solve a mystery through clever undercover sleuthing and fine intuition.'

Julia liked to think of herself as a clever, intuitive person, with measured insights into human nature. She had, after all, had years of exposure to the vagaries of the human heart and human behaviour. Her friends and colleagues regularly turned to her for wisdom and insight.

But it seemed she'd been wrong about Derek Pottington-Smith.

They reached the car and got in. Tabitha buckled up her seat belt and continued where she'd left off, gabbling away in excitement. 'Diane Keaton could play you in the movie, you look just like her. Hmm, maybe Viola Davis for me? In my dreams. Anyway, I feel a bit bad about wasting Ling's time. The way we asked all those questions, the poor thing probably thought she was going to sign up two new members today.'

'Yes, I feel a bit bad about that too. But it was for a higher purpose. Proving – or as it turned out, *dis*proving – the man's alibi for last Wednesday morning. So it seems Derek lied to Hayley about his whereabouts that morning.'

'Did he kill Mr Schofield then, do you think?'

'I can't see why else he would lie about being at the gym at that time. He must have lied to give himself an alibi for the time Schofield was killed.'

'You still don't seem convinced.'

'I don't know, Tabitha, it's just my gut feeling, really. I didn't peg him as a killer, but as you know, I've been very wrong before.'

'Yes, you were wrong about that poor lady with the kids and the nasty neighbours. But, Julia, you've been right many more times. You've made many good decisions and helped a lot of people. Don't be so hard on yourself.'

'Thanks, my friend, I just hadn't seen him as the murderer. Yes, he is big and tough and has a scary-looking dog, but in my experience that means very little when it comes to violence. You know, those built-up, gymmed-up types are usually more interested in developing their muscles than actually using their muscles to harm people. Let alone kill them.'

Julia turned on the car and made sure that her phone was connected to the Bluetooth. She would have to phone Hayley and give her the news about Derek's dodgy alibi. Once the phone was set up, she carefully pulled out of the parking place. Only when she was safely on the road did she continue her Big Man Theory. 'And let me tell you, some of the most cruel and dangerous men I've come across in my career were weaselly little blokes.'

In her head, she ran through some of the really nasty men she'd come across – the domestic abusers, the mean drunks who hit their kids after a few too many, the bullies. It wasn't at all an appealing line-up, but it was a varied one. Thugs came in all shapes and sizes.

Hayley's number rang and rang and went to voicemail.

'Could you do me a favour?' Julia asked Tabitha. 'Could you photograph the timetable and send it to Hayley?'

'Of course.' Tabitha took the sheet of paper, balanced it across her knees, and photographed it with Julia's phone. She sent the photograph to Hayley, and said, 'Should I send a message too?'

'I suppose so. Just say, "Passed the gym on my errands this morning and picked up this timetable. Take a look at Wednesday times."'

Tabitha typed it out laboriously – making mistakes, deleting and retyping. Julia didn't take her eyes off the road, but she could hear the little clicks from the phone and the little sighs and clucks from her friend. She tried not to be impatient. Tabitha finally sent it off. 'There you go. Sent.'

'Thanks.'

The phone was still in Tabitha's hands when it rang some minutes later, interrupting a conversation about the challenges of growing lemons. 'It's Hayley,' Tabitha said, looking at it as if it were a small hand grenade rather than a mobile phone. 'I hope she's not irritated. Maybe you should...'

Julia accepted the call via the car's Bluetooth. 'Hello, Hayley. Can you hear me? I never know with this car speaker.'

'I can hear you just fine. You went to the fitness centre?'

'I was with Tabitha. We've been on a little tour of the area and went to The Lemon Café for brunch – that new place over on the road to Edgely?'

Hayley grunted, one harsh monosyllable that managed to express familiarity with the establishment, complete disinterest in Julia and Tabitha's brunching adventures, and mild irritation at the whole escapade.

'They do a good breakfast. We took a walk around after, and

wouldn't you know that the Riverclub Fitness Centre is right there? We popped in.'

'You popped in, did you? To the very self-same gym Derek works at.'

'It was pure coincidence that we happened to be right next to it. Honestly, I had no idea it was there. We saw it there and actually Tabitha and I had been talking about upping our fitness game.'

Julia blushed to hear herself using the term which she'd winced at when she'd heard it out of the purple-painted lips of Ling the Membership Consultant. Tabitha raised her eyebrows in mock horror.

'We had thought about maybe joining a gym, so we went in to have a look and chat to a consultant. She showed us the timetable and when I saw Derek's name, I realised...'

'Well, it's good intel,' Hayley said grudgingly. 'It seems Derek wasn't where he said he was that morning, seeing as the boxercise class is in the afternoon. I tried to phone him, but it went straight to voicemail. I've sent Walter to his place to see if he's there. He's got some explaining to do. Meantime, we'll be getting a warrant to search the house.'

'Right, well, I hope it's...' Julia was going to say 'successful' but it didn't sound right, so after a brief pause she came up with: 'illuminating.'

'It had better be. I've got the regional director breathing down my neck. A new fellow with lots to prove. Two educators murdered within a week of each other has got "tabloid fodder" written all over it. The bosses are threatening to send down some crack team of investigators next week if I don't get this situation sorted out pronto.'

'You have an excellent track record; that sounds unnecessary and a bit unfair. And quite stressful for you, with all you've got on your plate as it is.'

'I know, right? Trying to solve the crime and watch my back

at the same time. On top of my usual case load. But it looks like this one's almost in the bag. Once I get that warrant and get Derek talking, we should be able to have it all wrapped up. Get the killer off the streets. And the brass off my back.'

29

Hayley seemed in good spirits for a woman who was going to spend the evening discussing dustbins and dementia at a village residents' meeting in an unflatteringly over-lit church hall. She'd given Julia a friendly wave and saved a seat for her next to her own in the row of six, second from the front. There were a few more rows behind, perhaps thirty seats in all.

'Derek Pottington-Smith is in custody,' Hayley said as Julia joined her, her voice low, but unmistakably tinged with pride. 'He's being held for questioning, and I've just heard we've got a search warrant for his house. They're going to search now. I couldn't get out of this meeting, so Walter is overseeing it, God help us all.'

The chairman of the Residents' Association, Flo's husband Albert, had arrived, and was bearing down on them like a tugboat in choppy waters.

'Don't mention the Smith thing,' Hayley muttered to Julia. 'I'm keeping it quiet for now.'

'Well, hello there, Captain,' Albert boomed.

'It's Detective Insp—'

'Congratulations! I hear you have the killer behind bars!'

Hayley went white and then red and then white again, and was, for once, struck dumb. Not that it mattered, because Albert was taking care of all the talking. 'Flo said the arrest was the talk of the Buttered Scone. A boxing fellow, they say. Derek Potter, something like that, was it? Don't know him myself, but Flo said Wilma's cousin knew him. Big fellow. Terrible, just terrible. But well done on cracking the case.'

'Thanks,' Hayley said reluctantly. 'But...'

A small crowd had gathered by this point and there was a lot of oohing and aahing and a bit of commentary and lots of questions.

'Did this boxer kill both of them? Or just one?'

'It was David Schofield he killed, I heard.'

'No, I heard it was Mrs Benjamin who was his victim.'

'It was Derek Pottington-Smith. Do you know, I was at school with him...'

'But why would he...?'

'And how...?'

'I'm not at liberty to confirm or deny, or to give out any information at this time,' said Hayley stiffly.

'Quite right,' said Albert, giving her an exaggerated sly wink and tapping his nose. 'Not a word. We know nothing. Now, take your seats everyone, and let's get to the other business.' He took his position at a small table in the front of the room, with his deputy chairperson, Nicky, at his side. He called Hayley up to sit in the third chair at the table, which she did reluctantly, shooting Julia a desperate glance as she did so. It did seem like rather a big showing of officialdom for a gathering of twenty people.

Jim McEnroe slid in next to Julia in Hayley's vacated seat, a notebook in his hand as if to proclaim his status as local journalist. 'Hey,' he said. 'I heard the news. Derek Pottington-Smith.'

'Did you know him?' Julia asked, as the rest of the crowd found seats and settled down.

'No.'

'Why did he send you the letter then, I wonder? Or do you think the letter was unrelated?'

'I don't know. I guess if it was him, he saw my name in the paper and thought he might as well send it to a specific person.'

'I suppose so.' Julia thought about it. It was always possible that the letter and the murder were unconnected, despite the threat. 'What are you doing here, Jim?'

'Um, covering important local issues.' Jim reddened. 'Seeing as my plan to break the big crime story didn't work out.'

'There's still a story there.'

'Well, *I* didn't work things out, but I'm hoping DI Gibson will give me the first interview, seeing as we...'

'Right! Settle down,' Albert bellowed. 'As you know, this is a special meeting to discuss the issue of the dustbins.'

A tall woman came in and sat herself right in front of them, almost completely blocking Julia's view. She rolled her eyes at Jim, who shrugged and muttered under his breath, 'It's like every concert I have ever been to. Some giant geezer pogoing in front of me.'

Albert started by recapping the events of the previous meeting. There was an incredibly tedious discussion about the thorny bushes on the side of Peony Lane and who should be removing them, followed by what seemed to be an insolvable debate about a blind rise a mile outside the village.

'Oh move on already, what are you going to do about the dustbins?' someone shouted from the back, which ended the pointless debate fairly effectively. A rumble came from fellow victims of the Rubbish Rummager.

'Yes, let's move on to the dustbins now,' said Albert. 'Now, everyone here is in the same boat. You've all had your dustbins messed with. But it's a delicate matter, on account of Edna being, you know... Well, you know how she is, Auntie Edna...' The bluster had rather gone out of him.

There was a sort of mumble, given that everyone did, in fact, know Auntie Edna.

'It is a mess though,' said a quiet woman at the back. 'And not very hygienic.'

'And who wants their rubbish all over the road for everyone to see?'

Heads craned to the right. Julia's followed. They were all looking at a woman at the far end of the first row of seats, who blushed furiously and said, 'I had people over for dinner. It's not as if I drank all those bottles of wine myself!'

'Nina, the wine bottle skittle lady, I presume,' Julia whispered to Jim, who looked mystified both before and after her explanation.

'What about the police – can't you do something?' came another voice.

Albert looked at Hayley expectantly. Julia could actually see Hayley sighing inwardly as she prepared to answer. She stood up. 'To be quite honest, I don't believe this is a job for law enforcement. We're not going to arrest Edna, obviously.'

'But we can't just let her carry on like that,' said the tall woman in front of Julia. 'It's a pain to clean up every time, if nothing else.'

'I agree, it's not ideal,' Hayley said patiently. She seemed all out of ideas, but then she looked at Julia and brightened. 'Julia Bird is a retired social worker, and a resident of our village. Maybe she has some ideas for how we could tackle this problem in a compassionate and effective manner. Julia?'

Julia was astonished to be called on and put on the spot. 'Gosh, well, yes. Hello, everybody. Well, my first thought is that Edna is a member of our community and we need to keep that in mind.' There was a murmur of approval. 'She is old, as we'll all be soon enough...' There was a ripple of tittering. 'And she deserves our kindness.'

A few people interjected 'Yes' or 'Right'. A couple more

made disgruntled harrumphing sounds.

Julia thought for a moment, racking her brains for solutions. Could they talk Edna out of her antics? Get her to change her route somehow? Learn acceptance? She had an idea: 'I do have one suggestion, which might be helpful.'

The audience turned towards her expectantly. You could hear a pin drop as they waited for her insight.

'You can each buy a bin lock. It's not expensive. People use them to keep the foxes out. You could lock your bins, and unlock them on dustbin day.'

There was a surprised silence at that suggestion, and then some affirmative nodding and muttering.

'Excellent idea! I consider the matter resolved.' Albert beamed from his place at the table 'We've done good work this evening, friends. There's sherry and biscuits at the back of the hall. I declare this meeting closed!'

'Nice work.'

'Thanks for dropping me in it,' Julia said, somewhat irritated at Hayley, but also pleased at the unanimous appreciation of her excellent suggestion, which of course was only practical and had nothing to do with social work at all.

Jim came up to join the throng by the sherry table. Julia introduced him to Hayley, who addressed him in her direct manner: 'I'm glad you're here. I've got something to ask you, with regards to this murder investigation.'

'Sure,' he said. 'And I've got something to ask you, too.'

'I need the original of that anonymous letter that you received about St Martin's. We've got a strong suspect and it would be very useful if his handwriting matches that note. More than useful. Blow the trumpets, sound the cymbals.'

'Yes of course, I'll bring it to the station tomorrow, shall I?'

The tall woman in the green coat, who had been blocking

their view earlier and was in front of them now too, turned around to face them. 'Jim McEnroe?' she said.

'Oh, hello. Marion, isn't it?' he said, recognising her. 'I didn't see you there.'

There was an awkward moment while they looked at each other. 'Um, this is DI Hayley Gibson, and this is Julia Bird.'

'Hello,' Marion said in a low voice, offering a hand to Julia, who winced a little at her firm-bordering-on-bone-crushing shake, and then to Hayley. A minute grimace crossed Hayley's face at the handshake too.

'How's the gym going?' Jim turned to the others and explained, 'Marion helped me on a story. Women's weightlifting in the Cotswolds. It's big, apparently.'

'It's going very well,' Marion said, reaching for a glass of sherry. 'In fact, I might have another story for you. A hot one. Front page stuff, I'd say.'

Jim looked pleased and embarrassed and a little flustered at her turn of phrase and said, 'Well, in that case, we should talk.'

'No time like the present.' Marion tossed her head towards the edge of the hall. Hayley and Julia watched them walk away with their little glasses, Marion's glass slightly dwarfed by her large hands, moving to an empty corner where they huddled, heads together in conversation.

'Well, I never,' said Julia. 'Did we just witness a pick-up?'

'I have no idea, although I doubt it. You know, I've seen that woman before. She's quite distinctive looking, isn't she? She was in the head's office at St Martin's, when I went to see Schofield. She's a mum at the school I think, so presumably not looking to pick up young men at town meetings.'

'For a detective, that's a big assumption. She could be divorced. Or in an open marriage. That's a thing these days, you know.'

'Who knows? You may be right. It's a mysterious world we live in.'

'It certainly is,' said Julia, watching Jim and Marion down their sherries with purpose. Marion looked towards the door of that hall. Jim followed her gaze. There was another brief exchange, she took out her car keys, and they started to move towards the door together.

'Well blow me down, it looks like you're right,' said Hayley. 'They do say opposites attract.'

The odd couple stopped. Marion went to say goodbye to Albert. Jim came over, giving Julia a wave and a grin as he approached. 'I'm going home. Marion's got a story for me, a big one.'

'Bigger than bins?'

'She won't say here, she wants to talk in private. No time like the present, as she says. She's coming over to my place.'

'Ah, a scoop!'

'Yeah, I hope so. See you around, Julia. I'll drop the letter off tomorrow, DI Gibson.'

Jim trotted to catch up with Marion. Julia watched them go. With his long shaggy hair and his slim build, Jim was indeed the opposite of Marion, with her strong, almost masculine body, the broad shoulders and the close-cropped head. Her green coat swayed with her swagger when she walked, Jim trotting alongside.

'I'll get going too,' said Julia to Hayley. 'Long day.'

'Good idea. I'll come out with you. I'll just say a quick goodbye.'

When they exited the hall, the odd couple were getting into a big BMW SUV. Marion held the door open for Jim, then went round to the driver's side and got in. Between Marion's tall build, Jim's slighter frame, and Marion's traditionally male action of opening the door for Jim, from a distance you would have guessed that Marion was the man and Jim the woman. Sometimes, thought Julia, things are not what they first seem.

As Marion started the big BMW, Julia had the distinct

feeling of something clicking into place. Marion and Jim. The car. She was sure she'd seen it before.

'Hayley,' she said, grabbing the detective's arm. 'How sure are you about Derek as a suspect?'

'Well, he denies it, of course, and there are certainly pieces missing, but there's a lot pointing to him. And we don't have another bloke in our sights, do we?'

'What if it wasn't a bloke? What if it was a woman?'

'A woman?' Hayley sounded like this was the most preposterous idea she had ever heard.

'The shoes. The strength. A big, tall woman?'

'I suppose...'

'We've made an assumption that isn't necessarily true. I was looking at that Marion woman and Jim, and I thought, well, a woman could have had the power and the height. Marion's feet must be at least a nine, maybe a ten.'

'You're right, it *could* have been a woman. But still, a man's more likely.'

But in Julia's head, the dominoes started to fall.

She remembered where she'd seen the car – on the security video, narrowly missing Marcus on the road from Edgely. The road to David Schofield's house. The person she'd seen getting out of the car hadn't been a man as she'd supposed, but a big woman in a long coat. A long green coat, similar to one that Julia had noticed on a woman that day at the fair. No. Not similar, thought Julia, squeezing her eyes tight and picturing the scene again. The woman she'd seen comforting her teenage son had been stooped down, wearing that very green coat.

And if Marion was the one who had nearly driven into Marcus, she'd immediately set off in the direction of Mr Schofield's house at just the time that the murderer might have done.

'Hayley. I think it's her... Marion.'

'Julia, you can't be accusing people just because they're big and tall. I'd be sent on diversity training if I did that!'

'Listen, Hayley. She's a mum at the school, so she would have known both victims, right?'

'Yes, but that's not enough.'

'I noticed her at the fair, too. She was there with a boy. She was in that same coat!'

'And she knew that I was at the school talking to Mr Schofield,' said Hayley, finally, it seemed, agreeing with Julia. 'The day before he was killed.'

'Yes,' said Julia. 'She would have known that there was a danger he would tell you that *she* had complained about Ursula Benjamin.'

Nicky interrupted them on the way to the door. 'Off so soon, ladies? A bunch of us are going for a pizza if you want to come. The Rubbish Victims support group needs carbs and wine, it seems. They're itching for an outing. Come along! Gosh, it's a pity that we just thought of it. Marion Smith already left with your journalist friend, and she's a party animal – but I always say...'

Julia turned away from Nicky in full steam, and said to Hayley. 'Smith! You cleared *Mr* Smith – but not *Mrs*. Hayley, it's her! She's on the rubbish route, so Edna could have found the scarf in her rubbish.'

'Julia, if you're right, we need to find them. Jim might be in danger. I think she's after the letter.'

'The letter! Yes, it would be in her handwriting, if our theory about that is right.'

'Let's go. Do you know where Jim lives?'

'I do. The little yellow cottage on Melody Avenue! Come on!'

'So, are you coming for drinks and pizza?' said Nicky, trying again. 'Because I always say...'

But they didn't hear what Nicky always said. They were already heading for the door.

30

'I'll go first. Stay behind me.'

Julia followed Hayley round the side of the cottage. The sun had gone down but there was still a faint glow to the evening sky. Hayley had called for backup, but there was no time to wait. They made their way carefully past the shrubs, as silent as they could be. Every crackle of twig sounded like a gunshot, to Julia's ears. She took long, slow breaths to calm her heart, which was careening about her chest like a bird in a cage.

They reached the end of the wall, where it met a little patio. Hayley peered round and returned to her position behind the wall. 'They're not outside, but it looks like they were here just minutes ago,' she said.

Julia slid part of her face and one eye past the end of the wall. Two candles flickered in two ruby-coloured glass jars. Two tumblers contained a golden liquid, perhaps whisky, poured over ice cubes. A blue plate held a wedge of soft cheese, a pile of crackers and a knife. The sliding glass door was open. They must have gone into the house.

'Cosy scene. Romantic lighting, snacks and all,' Julia whispered, returning to position. 'Maybe they went inside to get acquainted somewhere more comfortable.'

A look of mild disgust passed over Hayley's face. 'Thanks for that image. Well, I don't want to interrupt whatever's going on in there. I'll go round the front and knock on the door.'

'I have to say, this doesn't look like a dangerous situation,' said Julia. 'Perhaps I was wrong. Again.'

A loud exclamation interrupted her. 'Hey!' It was Jim's voice, loud, coming through the little window nearest Hayley and Julia. 'What are you doing poking around in my desk?'

'I'm looking for a pen; I want to make some notes. For the story,' said Marion Smith, her deep voice calm.

'You weren't looking very hard. The pens are right there in the jar.'

'I didn't notice. I was distracted by our... electricity...' Marion's low voice ended on a husky, throaty note that made Julia roll her eyes in the dark. The woman was putting on a show all right.

She looked at Hayley to see what she would do. Would she call out? Go in? Hayley put her finger to her lips and then held her hand up. *Quiet. Wait.*

'What's that in your hand?'

There was a moment of silence before Marion spoke again. 'It's not what it looks like.' Marion's voice sounded slightly panicked, less seductive.

'Well, it looks like... It's the letter! The anonymous letter about St Martin's I got at the paper. Did you hear me talking to the policewoman?'

'You're right. I did. I overheard. I just wanted to see it for myself, this key piece of evidence. The whole case is so intriguing, poor Mrs Benjamin. And Mr Schofield. And you were so clever, working it all out. You and the police, solving the crime, getting that dangerous Derek behind bars. I just wanted a peek.' The sexy voice was back.

Hayley and Julia waited. It was like listening to a soap opera. What would Jim do next?

'I think that you should just put the letter down and leave.' His voice sounded hurt and disappointed.

'Jim, it doesn't have to be this way. Let's go back to our drinks, enjoy the evening. Get to know each other.'

This Marion was a piece of work!

'No, Marion. You just came here for that letter. I don't understand why, but I'm not going to drink with you. Or work with you on a story. Or do... anything else with you. I don't trust you. You're up to something.'

Another moment of silence. You could almost hear Marion recalculating her moves.

'I'm sorry about that, Jim,' she said eventually. 'Really, really sorry.'

She didn't sound sorry, to Julia's ears. She sounded dangerous. Julia looked at Hayley, whose hand came up again. *Wait.*

There was a moment's silence. Julia felt the dull throb of foreboding in her bones, and wished fervently that she could see around corners or through walls. She didn't have to wait long. A crash broke the quiet night air, followed by a yell.

No more waiting. Hayley led the charge onto the patio and into the open French door, with Julia behind her.

Jim was on his back on the floor. Blood poured from a wound on his forehead. Marion was astride him, clutching a piece of paper in her left hand and a heavy glass jar in her right. Pens lay strewn on the carpet.

'Police!' Hayley shouted, hurling herself at Marion, just as the larger woman raised her hand, preparing to bring it down a second time on Jim's head. Hayley grabbed her from behind. Julia lunged forward and pulled the jar from her grasp.

Hayley pulled at Marion, trying in vain to get her off Jim, who was groaning and struggling to breathe. She couldn't shift her. Julia dropped the pencil jar, which splintered into shards of glass, and went to help Hayley. Between them, taking one side each, they managed to shift Marion and lift her enough for Jim to breathe and wriggle out from under her. She thrashed madly in their arms, shouting, 'You don't know what you're doing, you stupid man!' and 'Get off me, you mad cow!'

An elbow connected with Julia's eyebrow, sending a stab of pain and a bright sprinkling of stars shooting behind her eyes. It struck her that someone could get properly hurt in this melee, and that she herself was far too old to be in a fight. But she had no choice but to hang on as the bigger woman bucked and bellowed. Hayley had made a similar determination, and had Marion gripped firmly across the shoulders and neck with one arm. Hayley's other arm flailed at her jacket pocket and Julia hoped against hope that there was a taser in there and that she'd get her hand on it soon. She doubted the two of them could hang on and restrain the woman much longer.

Meanwhile, Jim had scooted far enough back to free his legs. A foot shot out and connected with Marion's jaw. For the first time, she paused in her writhing and shouting. Julia and Hayley pulled in unison, sending her crashing onto her back on the floor. Not knowing what else to do, Julia sat down on her. She knew she wouldn't be able to keep Marion down for long, but she hoped it would give Hayley time to get whatever it was out of her pocket. Jim added his weight to hers, and it seemed Marion was tiring or losing heart. All three were still for a minute and caught their breath.

But Marion gave a mighty heave, sending Jim and Julia scattering to the ground. She got up to her full height, letter triumphantly in hand, and gave a deep roar of triumph.

'You think you can stop me...'

She vaulted over Julia and out to the patio, the letter in her outstretched arm. Hayley was no more than two steps behind her, holding something black and solid in her hand. The paper fluttered over the candle, the flame catching the edge of it and throwing a golden glow upwards, illuminating Marion from below and throwing monstrous shadows up her face. She took on a frightening, ghostly look, her triumphant grin an awful grimace.

Her triumph lasted only a moment. Hayley reached out with her taser and a crackling, zapping sound was followed momentarily with a howl of pain or anger or both. Marion crashed backwards into a chair and fell in a sprawl onto the decking, the flaming paper still in her hand.

Julia was back on her feet, unsteady but upright. She couldn't think about the places that hurt, she just needed to get to that paper. She made it, stamping out the flame before it consumed the whole letter. Jim came rushing over and grabbed it off the ground, before Marion got any ideas, but she was limp now, tired and beaten. Hayley strode forward and clipped her handcuffs to Marion's wrists.

'Marion Smith, I am arresting you for the murder of David Schofield. You do not have to say anything. But it may harm your defence if you do not mention when questioned something that you later rely on in court. Anything you do say may be given in evidence.'

31

'That looks painful. Are you all right?' Julia asked, pointing to the bruise on Jim's forehead. It was purple and swollen, the edges already starting to turn a muddy green. A nasty cut at the centre was held together with medical tape.

He reached up and gave it a gentle prod. 'It's a bit tender, but not too bad. Dr O'Connor checked me out. No concussion, nothing broken, it will heal in its own good time. And you?'

He, in turn, pointed to the bruise that had flowered where Marion's elbow had connected with Julia's eyebrow.

She stepped back, ushering him into the house as she answered, 'I'm fine, thank you. It's not too sore.' Like him, she touched her bruise gingerly, oddly intrigued by its puffiness and tenderness. 'Who'd have thought I would get my first shiner in my sixties? I look as if I've done a few rounds with Derek Pottington-Smith, but Sean says there's nothing to worry about. Come on through. Hayley has just arrived. We're in the garden.'

She led him through the kitchen and out to her little patio, where Sean and Hayley were sitting at a table spread with cheeses and olives, crisps and a baguette, a bottle of sparkling water and a bottle of Chardonnay. Jake was under the table, his head on his paws, sleepy, but with his eyes open a slit, on the lookout for any stray crisps that might find their way to the floor.

Sean got up from his chair as they came out, put his hand on Jim's shoulder and shook his head. 'Keeping the doctor busy, you two are. Feeling all right?'

Jim smiled and nodded and sat down next to Julia. He dropped his reporter's notebook on the table, a pen held tightly in its spiral binding.

Hayley looked at the two of them wryly. 'You shouldn't go out in public together; people will think the two of you have been in a fight with each other.'

'I'm not going out again for a day or two,' Julia said. 'I got some funny looks at Second Chances this morning, I can tell you.'

'You went to work?' Jim said. 'After everything you've been through this weekend?'

'Julia is very reliable,' said Sean, with pride. 'Didn't want to let them down.'

'I wasn't there long. Wilma said I would scare the customers. She insisted I go home. After pumping me for gossip, of course. Anyway, I feel fine.'

'You're both lucky, but I'd advise no more fighting.' Sean used his earnest doctorly tone, which Julia found endearing.

'There shouldn't be much cause for fighting. Marion is going to be a guest of His Majesty for a while, I should think,' said Hayley. She might have been the only one to escape the confrontation without a visible injury, but Julia could see that she looked wiped out, dark rings under her eyes standing out against her pale face. 'The evidence is lining up. For a start, the handwriting on the letter sent to Jim matches Marion's.'

'Now you'll fill us all in on that in a moment, but let's get Jim a drink first,' said Julia.

'You sit, I'll do it,' said Sean. 'What'll you have, Jim?'

'Water to start, please.'

Sean played host, handing Jim a glass of water and pushing a bowl of crisps in his direction. It was a balmy evening, the first night that spring that it had been warm enough to sit out in the last of the light in just a thin sweater. The air was fragrant with the smell of the gardenia bush, and the chickens made the soft contented clucking sounds of them settling in for the night. The gathering had something of the air of a picnic or a garden party, except that two of the guests were sporting lurid and painful injuries, and the talk was of murder.

'Did you get hold of Bernard Smith? What did he say?' Julia asked, eager to get the full story from Hayley. Jim picked up his notebook and took the pen from the spiral binding. He raised his eyebrows inquiringly at Hayley.

'Off the record for now,' she said. 'I'll give you a proper interview when I've cleared it with higher up.'

'Right,' said Jim, closing his notebook. 'First interview? Exclusive?'

'Yes. So, the poor man was in a terrible state. He was already on the plane on his way home when we tried to contact him. He knew nothing of what had been going on, and he came back to the country to find a uniform officer at the arrivals gate at Heathrow, and his wife in police custody. We brought him straight into the station. He arranged a lawyer, of course. We did a preliminary interview, just for some background.'

'What did he say about the boy?' Julia asked. 'I've been so worried about him.'

'The boy's name is James. He's staying with an aunt. As you suspected, he'd been victimised by Ursula Benjamin. He isn't a very robust chap, by all accounts. It says here' – she opened a brown paper file that lay on the table in front of her – 'that he didn't want to go to school; he became fearful and anxious. Marion Smith took him to a psychologist, who told her the problem was at school, with the teacher, and she should work with the school to find a solution, or move the child.'

'She chose neither of those options,' Julia said, sadly. 'And now the child is worse off than ever.'

'Well, from what the husband says, they did complain to Schofield, but he didn't do anything about it. Turns out, you were right. We spoke to Robert Benjamin about this part, and David Schofield had a bit of a fling with Ursula many, many years ago. So we think that she must've blackmailed Schofield into letting her stay – but we'll never know that part for sure. Anyway, he made a few empty promises – also suggested the child get medication for his anxiety – but didn't act. Ursula was due to retire this year so they decided to wait it out. It was only a few more months.'

'So what changed?' asked Julia.

'Well, this part I got from Marion herself. She heard via the school mum grapevine that the head was trying to get Ursula Benjamin to stay on for another year or two. Once Marion heard that the contract was likely going to be extended, she couldn't bear it. She was furious.'

'When was this? When did she get that news from the Car Park Mafia that set her off?' Julia asked.

'The week before the fair, apparently. And then the boy saw Mrs Benjamin at the fair and he started freaking out. He wanted to go home. Really lost it, apparently.'

Julia remembered seeing the two of them, the tall woman and the teenage boy, the mother trying to comfort her son. Little did she know at the time, she'd seen a woman who would, within the hour, commit murder. 'Poor James. And poor Marion, seeing him so sad and anxious.'

Hayley looked only marginally convinced. 'More awful for Ursula Benjamin and her family,' she said, shortly. 'I've filled Robert in on the latest developments. He's shocked, of course. Luke is in a bad way, dealing with his own regrets around his relationship with his mother. It's awful.'

'Of course. The whole situation is tragic. There's no excuse for what Marion did.'

'Marion saw Ursula and decided to talk to her, one-on-one, rather than through the school and the headteacher. She saw her across the fields. Told James to go and wait in the car and went to speak to her. According to her, she was angry, impatient, but not out of control. She just wanted to convince Mrs Benjamin that it was time to go. Ursula was having none of it. She gave her the brush-off, wouldn't listen to her, just said some none-too-complimentary things about her and her son, and walked off.'

'Into the maze...' said Julia. 'And Marion followed her?'

'Yes. Marion claims she had no intention of killing her, just wanted to convince her to take retirement. But her anger got the better of her. She threatened the woman, said she was working with a journalist on a story about her behaviour and the school's neglect.'

'If you consider delivering an anonymous letter to the paper "working with a journalist" I suppose that's close to the truth,' said Jim.

'Well, Mrs Benjamin treated her with utter disdain. She turned her back on Marion, sat down on the bench and ignored her completely.'

'And that's when Marion strangled her.' A vision of the dead woman came to Julia in shocking clarity – her sensible haircut and little gold hoop earrings, the basket on the bench. Behind the bench, Julia's mind's eye inserted the imposing figure of Marion Smith in her green coat, looking down on Ursula, her strong hands on the striped scarf, pulling tighter and tighter. It was such a violent image, she could hardly believe it had happened.

'She took the scarf, and Ursula's handbag,' said Hayley. 'She said that she wasn't thinking straight and thought somehow we might not be able to identify Ursula without the bag. And then she threw them both away – which was how Edna came to have the scarf. No sign of the bag – Edna doesn't seem to have it, so I suppose it's sitting on a rubbish dump somewhere.'

Julia tried to get her head around it all. So much anger. So many irrational decisions.

'I can imagine her anger and pain, but from there to strangling another person from behind... I don't know. Is there a history of violence? Or irrational behaviour? Any diagnosis that might make sense of it?'

'Well, according to her husband, there *was* something. In the last few months he'd noticed certain changes in her personality. He said she'd always been impatient. She was an only child who had never really been good at sharing or waiting her turn or not having her own way.'

The words stirred something in Julia's brain – 'impatient... only child...' The graphologist's handwriting analysis! Julia looked at Hayley to see if she had also recognised the words that had reduced the two of them to hysterical laughter in the car.

Hayley was too busy with her story, it seemed, to catch the wide-eyed look from her friend, or the little twitch of a smile. 'In the last few months he'd started noticing that she seemed angrier than usual, more reactive. She admitted to us that she'd started taking steroids soon after she'd started weightlifting, to build up her strength and muscles.'

Sean broke in, 'It's a known side-effect of steroid misuse or overuse. An increase in irritability and aggression, particularly if the user is taking high doses, or has existing anger issues. They call it "roid rage". It's well-documented.'

'It seems it might have been a contributing factor. The strange coincidence is that she was training with Derek Pottington-Smith. And buying the drugs from him too, it seems.'

'He was *dealing*?' said Jim, looking up from scritch-scratching away in his notebook.

'Yes. DC Farmer searched his house and found the steroids. That's why he didn't want me to come in and ask him questions that day. He offered to come down to the station instead, remember, Julia?' DC Farmer seemed to have forgotten that he wasn't supposed to have told Julia about this.

'Right, yes, of course. He said he had to feed the dog and the boy and he'd come straight away.'

'Which he did. Well, it seems he was selling to clients at the gym and he kept his stash at home.'

'Then why did he lie about the timing of the gym class?'

'I asked him the same question, Julia. He said it was just his instinct to give himself an alibi. The lie popped out of his mouth. I'm assuming he was going about his steroid business at the time.'

'And what happened to David Schofield? Did Marion Smith kill him, too?' asked Jim.

'At first she denied it. But when we matched her fingerprints to the prints on the golf club, she confessed. According to her, Mr Schofield asked her to come and see him. When we asked for the name of the parent who had complained, the school lawyers advised that the easiest route to giving the police her name was to just get her permission. He had no inkling that she was the murderer, so he thought she would easily agree. Instead, she panicked when he asked her, grabbed the golf club, and hit him. She claims she immediately realised that she'd made a terrible mistake – but it was too late – he was dead. So she tried to make it look like a random break-in.'

They sat in silence for a moment, each with their own thoughts. Julia's primary response was sadness. It was all so unnecessary. She couldn't help thinking, 'if only...' If only Ursula had been kinder, or David Schofield braver, or Marion more in control of her anger.

The sun had dipped below the horizon and the light and the temperature fell in tandem, almost instantly. 'It's getting a little chilly out. Shall we move inside?' asked Julia, rousing them from their contemplation.

'I'd best be going,' said Hayley. 'It's been a long day.'

There was a scraping of chairs as they stood up, and then the clinking of plates and glasses being gathered. Jake woke and got to his feet to position himself for any delicious morsel that might come his way during the clean-up. He looked at Julia with eyes like melting chocolate drops and in a moment of weakness she gave him a small crust of baguette.

Sean left shortly after the guests, prescribing a good night's sleep for Julia, and leaving her with a firm hug and a tender kiss.

Julia decided she would count the cheese and olives as supper and just have a cup of tea. She filled the kettle and put it on. While it hummed quietly on the stove and Jake snored gently in his bed, Julia sat at the kitchen table and let her mind wander over the evening's discoveries. Letting the details of the cases recede, she thought instead of Luke and James, the two boys now without their mothers. She thought of her own Jess, so far away, and felt a pang in her chest, an ache of loss and longing.

Getting up, she walked to the sitting room, sat at her roll-top desk and opened a small drawer. She took out the necklace she had bought at the Spring Fair for Jess's birthday, with its ancient curled fossil on the silver chain. Switching on her iPad, she started an email.

Dearest Jess

I've been thinking about what to do about your birthday. I found something that I think you'll love – it is rare and beautiful, like you. It's a two-part present, and the second part – assuming of course that this is what you want – is an air ticket home when the semester finishes in June. When you come, I'll tell you a strange and sorry tale of murder here in the village, and how your mother got involved in solving it.

Please say yes!

Love,

Mum

A LETTER FROM KATIE GAYLE

Dear reader,

More Julia Bird books are in the works. There are adventures aplenty for Julia, Jake and the colourful characters of Berrywick. If you want to keep up to date with all Katie Gayle's latest releases, just sign up at the following link. Your email address will never be shared and you can unsubscribe at any time.

www.bookouture.com/katie-gayle

Katie Gayle is, in fact, two of us – Kate and Gail – and we want to say a huge thank you for choosing to read *A Village Fete Murder*. We have loved exploring more of Berrywick with Julia and Jake. We hope that you have too. If you are a new friend of Julia Bird, please grab a copy of *An English Garden Murder* to read about Julia's first few weeks in Berrywick, and then *Murder in the Library* for more of her sleuthing.

You can also follow us on Twitter for regular updates and pictures of the real-life Jake! (Who is, if anything, even naughtier than Julia's Jake.)

We hope you enjoyed reading about Julia's adventures, and if you did we would be very grateful if you could write a review and post it on Amazon and Goodreads, so that other people can discover Julia too. Ratings and reviews really help writers!

You might also enjoy our Epiphany Bloom series – the first three books are available for download now.

You can find us in a few places and we'd love to hear from you – Katie Gayle is on Twitter as @KatieGayleBooks and on Facebook as Katie Gayle Writer. On Twitter, you can also follow Kate at @katesidley and Gail at @gailschimmel.

Thanks,

Katie Gayle

facebook.com/KatieGayleWriter
twitter.com/KatieGayleBooks

Made in United States
North Haven, CT
13 July 2023

38866642R00146